QUERENCIA WINTER 2024

Querencia Press
Chicago Illinois

CONTENTS

POETRY

Sun-Eater – Adam Paxton (he/him)

It's a Frankenstein pleasure.
A kiss crushed to atoms
In a confusion of strangled syllables.
You are mad scientist urges.
You sun-eater,
You who can see
A universe of fire diamond
In an infinitesimal speck of infant grit.
Pleasure on the shores
Of hostile oceans.
But you are no shoulder to cry on,
Just the fair in love and war.

The Day My Father Died – Adam Paxton (he/him)
—After Kerry Hardie

Only his sky fell.
We watched his eyes widen with fright
And saw him claw himself home to sanity
Through the wreckage of his life.
Crows stretched their bellies
Sensing a feast was in the offing.
We couldn't understand
How he'd only just realized
He was drowning;
He'd been drowning
Our entire lives.

So he made it to shore
Staring into the fire,
Huddled and vacant
Ever since.
He takes what they give him
And refuses to go to the shore
Anymore.
But we still look out to sea
And watch the Crows have their way.
To survive
He left so much of himself out there
He never really came back at all.

Swallowing the Blood – Mateo Perez Lara (they/them)

out the womb

pulled from mother's stomach

from skidded-open knee

stabbed deep thigh

first fuck

fistful of glass

a fist inside

of dog-bitten eye

man-bitten hand

friend's cycle

unwelcomed dick

his bad driving

his resentment, shameless

in this desecrated room of safety

consecrated mouth, with love, outgrown

on rough night, abandoned / earned

flurry of threats with gun & knife

through healing

through repentance

through forgiveness

through bitterness

in all unencumbered anger

in all unbridled thought of vengeance

in all this hope still pumping through

every last thick drop.

Milking a Viper – Mateo Perez Lara (they/them)

When he stepped in the room

I felt anxiety, a pearl necklace, through my unwavering body

felt no holiness, no monarch tendencies, I just stacked books

applied to jobs every few weeks, as he asked, made sure my
grandma knew I loved her

my god, how obedient I've become.

age does a tricky thing in the body, observance became the game,
and men

have no use unless I conjure one, if my green-red blood is any
veneration

I'm drawing pictures in hopes to conclude an undying obsession
with the past

It won't bring S back, it won't bring M back, it won't bring Papa
back, no men back

Even if I salt the room, even if I light the matches, recite what the
book says

Even if I prayed to God, even if I believed.

-

No rabbit's tail, no chicken beak, no toxin

Just you and I, just thoughts and I, just *another* year you and I.

-

They say don't tempt men, they say go back to submission, power is in the eye and the fist of the conqueror. The one who lived through history, the one who wrote it, the one with the glint in his eyes, a twitch in his pants, who didn't get to say what and when and where, must I bring the flute out, coax a venomous reminder from his tongue—

Writhe on the ground, he suckles air, he asks, "WHAT CAN YOU GIVE? WHAT DO YOU NEED?"

Shed your skin, shave off your edges, give me another place to hide, once you strike, I promise not to pry for the truth, you see that token dripping down my thigh—I wore the lingerie you like, I lied on my face, I stayed on my back, do you see what is throbbing, running down

dribbling from your lips, you said so yourself: *spill the whole world if you cannot dominate it—*

I will hold it deep inside, make relic out of your carelessness—

Did you know they used to worship you, King? Did you know that once you were all and now, at once, you will be nothing.

My Revenge is a Chainsaw – Mateo Perez Lara (they/them)

—buzzed straight into your abdomen, left a quivering token, I don't
wear many masks, just the one you see before you. But I will take
every man's face and reveal it as punishment for their crimes.
Would your shame feed a town, a city, a whole country, you look
into the mirror, smear on devil-red lipstick, wait for mother's cooing
/ calming embrace, she never existed, you never fracture a proper
limb, another year goes by, another anger, another man on the
hook, you stitch his lips together, you paint his cheeks a dirty pink,
why are we grabbing for a little morsel. Your mind is reverberating
with anguish so now you hear the rev, feel rage coming closer.

—through the forest, through the van, through the truck, speeding
down a bridge, I hide your mistakes in a vat of chili, you like this,
you revel in my obedience, not anymore, I am not friend, I am foe,
down the hatch, in the garden, across these cracked stairs, in your
field.

—months pass by, we haven't learned much yet, only how to seek
repentance, only vengeance in our rotten mouths, way down the
gut, I still sheen my blade, it purrs when I'm deep in your chest,
deep in your breast, where that little heart lies, I can't wait to taste
what love is really like, a little salt, a little vinegar.

No heart is saved. He severed the safety when he purred the car and stalled it in the front of my house. If I snuck out, I was his. If I stayed in, I belonged to the crevice of autonomy. He buried me in the earth, three days later like God, fully fledged I entered his body and tore through the town, overturned, and rebuilt his heart. He can't stand the sight of himself in the mirror all he sees is me and what he's done, what he cannot escape, what he can only agonize on.

Do You Want to Know About Mud Resolve? – Karen Keefe
(she/her)
> *CW: Trauma in childhood*

1.
The sound of my voice is a lie because you do not know
the simplest confession, I am not able to tell the real truth.

One night I packed a suitcase. It was small and brown. I was small
and my blue eyes saw two of everything. I walked out of my house
and away from its big windows, big trees, big sad. I sat at the end of
the street trying to ask the finches in the trees to wait for me, to
come with me, to help me dream up a different past where no baby
brothers died and I didn't need to try so hard to be good.

2.
Please understand if you really want to know me
I cannot speak up for myself, the words will not come out—there
really is a reason for this shameful behavior. An ambulance came in
the middle of the night. A mother gone. A father not returned. No
one to remind—being in third grade means I must have a fountain
pen today. When Philip has three how can I be in such trouble for
taking one, just for now? He is my friend. I would give it back.

Forgive me, teacher
I know I should have told you   something happened
and I should have remembered   use my words   ask him first
but what if he said no

3.
I don't want to tell anyone about all this
I did not remember it is a school day. All I can remember is the
ambulance, how I must now   Be Our Safety.

Forgive me, sister and brother
How do I tell you no one is coming? Is it a lie to protect you from the
truth?

This is where I am afraid it all becomes beyond forgiving
What would happen if you all, mother/father/teacher/beloved
knew how much worse it was/is:
yesterday's underwear beneath my skirt
only enough time to braid one sister's hair
apple juice crackers and some peanut butter for breakfast
but no lunch and no money to buy one for us.
I am now alone with your attention and what was never going to
happen
for me   to me   with me   because

4.
Therapy is being in the confessional box.
My therapist quickly decides she understands, I stand up and ask
her to come outside with me. We walk into the weeping woods
behind her house. I lie down behind a rock wall. This is where I wait
for my appointment. Look at this wall, the firmly stacked squared-
off base level all hidden by overgrown grass. Moon lichen grows all
over it.

I ask her will she sit down with me. Before I go back into that room
where her checklists are waiting to make sense of me, I need to

know for real—Am I visible here behind the wall when she looks out her ancient windows with their seeded glass, the hinge plates set just so?

And what does she know of mud resolve? What do I do with the mix of bones, stones, fallen trees, memories? My path blocked forward, back, all on top of me.

Invitation to a Breach in Time – Karen Keefe (she/her)
CW: Psychiatric Hospitalization

The locked fifth floor.
Summoned by your doctors
Family Meeting in the Psych Ward.
I arrived too early.

My eyes howl
at the memory sight of you folded small
on a chair.
You are outside of the meeting circle.
Shadowed by fluorescent light
hospital smells surround you.

A crowd of staff circles me.
I can only glimpse you
beyond their shoulders.

I hear the doctor's accusation,
why did I abandon you so many times?
I look at you
and fail—
to only pay attention
to you.
I feel on trial and accused
so much time is lost.

There is only one thing I need to do
address you, only you,
and risk three simple words,
"I am sorry".

I look at you
but you are looking
where nothing is left of us
but skin cells caught in sun shafts.

Looking back I knew – Dahra Perez (she/her)

Aphrodite sat next to me in my sixth grade classroom.

She had long brown hair and big black glasses that would have made anyone look ridiculous, but not her. In our PE class she wore our uniform like it was made for her and I told myself that everyone noticed how pretty she looked, it wasn't just me.

Aphrodite was a singer at my parents' wedding. She wore a suit and bright red lipstick. Her voice was soft and smooth and she looked at me and I felt special. I remember red cheeks, hidden smiles, and a purposely forgotten realization.

Aphrodite taught me how to cook. Soft hands that held mine as I held a knife and then a pan then a dish. The kitchen was always bustling with something new, and I convinced myself it was the cooking and the stove that made my body heat up, not anything else. Not the girl standing next to me, blue apron with a ribbon on its back.

We still carry it – Dahra Perez (she/her)

A man fell out of a window, *on fire*
My grandpa watched from the sidewalk
Plastic grocery bags hanging dumbly by his side
The fire did not go out
The man died.

He got home, put the groceries down
No greetings, no kiss on the cheek to his wife
He spent an hour in his room before joining for dinner
Did not speak about it,
Just moved on.

How many times did he watch something
On fire
And had to bear it in silence?

I look at my dad, so similar to him.
Did he ever see someone on fire?

Sunflower – Wanda Deglane (she/her)

It was mid-March
when I felt you
slip between my fingers.

I did not bleed. I was sick
every morning, the nausea arriving
in the back of my throat like
an unwelcome visitor. My hips ached,
and still I did not bleed. My boyfriend
was beside himself with fear.
You have to get rid of it.
This thing *will destroy us.* His eyes
stretched wide enough to see white
all around. His fists clenched.
His voice was far too loud. I saw then
what terror can do to a good man.
He kept calling you *it. Thing.*
He refused to see you as a *you*.
A bounty.

And then, before I knew
what to call you. Before I could
fight for you. You were gone.
A large, bright puddle in my dress.
It happened at work. I touched you.
There, not there. I imagined a little body.
Little fingers. I pictured you, a leafy seed
inside me, drowned. I cleaned
myself and then a client came,
and I had to anchor the scream

in my chest for the next hour. I came home,
pulled my mother aside. She said,
Oh, thank god. She said, *You didn't
want this, Wanda. Not now.* I slipped
into bed, quiet, sobbing, changed.

I knew then what I think
I always knew:
My body could never be a home.

I did want you. I wanted you
so much it made my teeth ache.

I didn't tell anyone then because
it felt silly. I wish I told everyone.
He would have hated me until the end of time.
Our relationship would not have lasted
another moon. My career would have
been put on hold, maybe forgotten forever.
My body would have been wrecked,
my meager finances depleted. And
I didn't care. I wanted you. I would
have given it all up with a swiftness.
I would have chosen you,
a million times over. I would have
loved you alone if it meant
I got to love you.

**A name is an heirloom, a breath you carry for generations –
Wanda Deglane** (she/her)

1. My names are odes for the women who came before me, songs of their greatest fears and triumphs. I live because they straightened their spines. I live because they loved me, more than the ground beneath their feet.

2. *Wanda*

   a. A princess, a witch, a fairy, an angelfish, a slender teenage tree.

   b. My first name was given to me as a gift by my grandmother, the sharpest, strongest, toughest woman I know. As a girl, I'd sit at her knee and listen to her stories of all the leering men she punched in the face.

   c. Sometimes at the dinner table, she gets in the mood to recount her many bruises. She drifts back to her mother, gnarled fingers and cruel fists. How even on her deathbed, her mother denied ever lifting a finger against her, instead said, *Wanda, you made me suffer. You have no idea the suffering you caused me.* How her father slapped her in the face for the last time when she was 19, and, trembling, she fumbled for the courage to say, *You're dead to me. You're nothing to me now.* How she fled and sobbed the whole bus ride to Juliaca because it was the first time she had ever left home.

   d. And she married a man who drank the last drop of every drink his lips touched. Who carved his name into her flesh with fists. Ground into the grooves of the floor, her vision fizzled to nothing. Her children ran crying for help.

   e. Even today, my grandmother only ever dresses in black. I think what I'm trying to say is, she's grieving something that still stumbles in my blood. What I'm trying to say is, she is tough because the world sharpened her with each brutal *thwick* of a blade.

3. *Elizabeth*

    a. A dozen queens and empresses, a writer, an actress, a cunning chess player. An oath, given by god.

    b. My middle name was given to me by my mother. It is her own middle name and the middle name of a dozen women in her family.

    c. My mother's father was a dishonest man. He'd lay with every woman in San Juan, come home with perfume on his neck and lies on his tongue. When he finally fucked off to the other side of town, my mother was left with too-small shoes and a dad-shaped void. My mother's mother never hugged her. Never touched her except with the handle of a broom. They lived in her grandparents' house, swimming in aunts and cousins. There was never enough money. Never enough food to go around. My mother tells me about selling her belongings on street corners. When they were desperate, my mother and her brother would ride the train across Lima to their father and ask for money. He'd press 10 soles into her palm and send her on her way.

    d. My mother immigrated to America when she was 18 years old, alone with a man she had been dating for a year and wasn't sure if she wanted to marry. The first of her family to leave behind her homeland. She was pregnant, carrying only her clothes and some salad bowls her mother sent. In the airport, she trembled and worried that someone would notice she was foreign. That she didn't belong. And clutching her bags, she heard a Gin Blossoms song over the loudspeakers. She didn't understand any English, but she imagined this white man was telling her, *Everything is going to be okay, Maria. You made it here. you saved yourself. You will save your family. Just settle in. Welcome home.*

4. Most of the time, a name is a wish. Long-winded and sore-kneed. A seasick desire. I hope that you live to carry me the way I carried you. I hope you grow sturdy as a tree and powerful as an oath. I hope life is kinder to you than it was to me. But more than anything, when the world comes with its stick to put you out of your misery, I hope you're strong enough to stand up. I hope you can face it. I hope you can live, in spite of it all.

Ode to the Opening Shot of Lady Bird – Wanda Deglane (she/her)
—After Lady Bird (2017) dir. Greta Gerwig

I wish my mother loved me
a little bit more or not at all. I wish
I could tear her apart with my teeth. I wish
she would just knock on my door and hold me.
We smile saccharine at each other now,
but we still know how to slice clean through
to the bone. My mother, my mirror. I could
kick my whole life on its side, change
my name and run off to someplace foreign
and green, and still all I'd be is a wretched
extension of her. Unwitting, unwilling,
I carry her hot blood, her cold shoulder,
her storm cloud. A slap across the face and
a too-tight dress. I remember being 3 years old
and bolting out of the bath, freezing cold and
dripping all over the floor, into my mother's
arms so she'd warm me up. It was the only time
she'd touch me. She knows which buttons
to push, and I know how to vomit up cruel-
father words. Pained silence, her footsteps
growing softer, quieter. Tentatively, we try
to rebuild. Conversations at the kitchen table
and chicken marsala. Her hands expertly
sprinkling the perfect amount of seasoning.
Mine still clumsy, unsure. She finally says,
I'm so sorry for the pain I've caused you. I didn't
know how to be a mother, how to split a thing from
my own child body and watch it molt into a smaller me.
I didn't know how to slam on the brakes, didn't see

you lying in the middle of the road. I say, *I love you*
with everything that I am but I'm terrified I'm only
doomed to become you. I turn her apologies
around in my hands. My trembling fingers
dance around the word *forgiveness*, new and shiny.
It's useless but I'm tired of hurting, tired of
my kicking and clawing retribution. Sometimes
I look into my mother's eyes and notice
how green they are as if it's the first time
I'm seeing them. Tiny tap dancing shoes
and sandwiches sold on the street corner.
Like children, we learn to speak gently,
to hold each other in the dark.

The Obligations – Dr. Manjusha Hari (she/her)

Hope could be written,
as an odd number.
It's like the sallow wordings,
the never ending waitings
or the molten life span.

The real but unforseen twists
of the time twirl
dejecting me and dragging me
to the forgetfulness
of my blind sea!
Its astonishing nights
and winter trickling mornings
are beat in me!

There is an obligation
between me and my illness.
It is written beneath the root tips
of time; The uninvited Enchanter—
How obdurate you are!
I will immolate my crust,
the blaze of my poetry
and the vastness of my verve!
For the Pacific sleep, you offered!

fall – Izzy Okonji (he/him)

my father told bedtime stories differently.

he told me about how delilah drank samson
          as a poison that was asleep in her

          belly until she ate inside a host of schadenfreude.

he told me not all stories were meant for kids.

he said   that there is a quicksand that swallows up a kid

          when he walks from his playground to a playing
          card of pluperfect history —

          this also means, he walks his own psyche into

          a street of psyches.

he wrote   psalms on every limb of the kitchen corners
          (our favorite places), fearing that his spoken word

          would be ricocheting ammos.

          written languages are crosshairs, he said.

he sank   his rod into the outskirts of his spine, & he began
          to shed tears using my grandfather's eyes the day

          i came back home with a nintendo game i stole
          from school—that day, my mother confessed to

the 1st time his palm fell to her face with a splash

like niagra. my elder brother got himself hurt by
text-messaging his girlfriends.

            his infidelity had leapt over his pillow. on saturdays,
he would   drive to a barbershop—on the mirror, all he could
            see were his bones.

he would   rev his engine to belch out his despondency

on the throat of his new girl. every night
he saw my mom was a shadow of winter

that he donned; her silence was a katana blade
brandishing—but, she still looked like the feet

of a burning haiku—beautiful.

his open eyes closed to his body's

length in a soil of his last memory, happened
right before my eyes.

all a live man could do is to escort his dead with
whiffs & prayers.

on hearing about his fall, my mom didn't go
apeshit; instead, she went bones, too.

Flipping Coins – Allison Rose-Paoli (she/her)

There is a small hole dug through and beneath the cold foundation of my blue room. I crawl into the opal space and into a fetal bind. I am a feral cat. Moving through my darkness cautiously, suspicious of every sound and shadow, of every ache beat relentlessly against my tired soul. Wool and coal wash over me. I try to meditate on the familiarity of grief. Grief for what was lost and what was never found. I am safe under the suffocation of regret. But the fabric of sadness itches at me. I am uncomfortable in my own skin. And with my thumping pulse. The walls lean closer. The air is stagnant. I try to brush away the grey matter settling across my eyes but my arm is too heavy to lift. I succumb to my old friend, loneliness. She never disappoints. Beside me, my younger self dances, and she smiles. She writes stories and loves animals. But hope was exorcised from her body in velvet time and I fall deeper into my hurt. The voices from beyond this sunken life make me wonder what it is like to be normal. To have friends. To fall in love. To feel purpose. To not feel everything all at once. But my abyss is Judas and I am seduced deeper into its vast solitude of vacancy. Doing time in life's cell of despair. It is hard to breathe here, but not hard enough.

Breath of Eyjafjörður – Natalie De Paz (she/her)

Generations of boats have followed
generations of whales, names passed down
along the ever-constant current.
The breath of a whale has as many meanings
as a yow on the in-breath.

To call a god a monster
is accurate, if biased.
Ingimar hands me a mug of hot chocolate, tells
me he is no longer indifferent about whale hunting.
He learned to love whales this summer, rare
and innumerable as the waves.
We count the slow minutes between surfacing,
waiting for a wish to come true.
Their sighs mark my heart, their tails mark the fjord
surface. Ingimar teaches us these portals are called flukeprints.

Mother and calf
sigh in unison, breathe in rhythm with each other
then collapse into perpetual canon.
Their bodies echo the shape
of the mountains that watch over us,
they form a smooth and perfect curve, pushing into the depths.
We fall silent to accept their spouted
blessings, their mist carried on the wind.

Sharing breath with the whales is a reminder of all we share, let
the mighty hope well up within.
The dog named Aska waits for us to dock, eases
the melancholy of being land-bound, left

with questions for the whales until we meet again.

Do they dance with the aurora on the water?
Do they name the mountains as the waves?
Do they sing of us as friends?

EVERY TIME I THROW AWAY A PIECE OF PLASTIC I FEEL UTTERLY POWERLESS – **Natalie De Paz** (she/her)

Exiting Aldi I feel pride at my savings,
Veering home with my usuals and my Aldi Finds. Are my
Eyes twitching because of too much screen time or stress?
Rude of me to pretend they're not linked like
Yesterday's sunset and today's ennui. I never stopped

Thinking ennui was cool. Despite their politics and work
In therapy, I do think
Most artists agree. It balances out because I believe in myself
Even though

It's absurd.

The cookies from most grocery stores come in clamshell plastic
Hinged boxes, clearly displayed in neat
Rows of six and six. I would honestly prefer a paper bag
Over this bullshit
We know none of it is recyclable. On the internet I learned

A term called
Wishcyclying, which is when
A person isn't sure if something is recyclable,
Yet they put it in the recycling with

A wish that it will indeed not be dubbed

Precious garbage.
Instead of wishcycling, we let our
Ever-full receptacle overflow dozens of times over into
Chaos,
Eventually taking the bins and boxes

Over to the recycling center that does more than our
Fair county deigns to do. We the

Peasants stare out in the mirrors across
Lacquered America,
And don't let them convince you it's
Self-destruction we see there. They won't tell you
They've been evil, all along,
In every way. Mark the tragic difference/distance between the jester & the
Clown.

I feel utterly powerless.

CLEANSE – Amanda M. Blake (she/they)

cleanse me mycelium
strip the toxic lining
within the extended hole
of my fleshly trunk
shift state of matter
render liquid from solid
make vegetable of animal
fungal food of friend
in concert with beetles
infest the hollow
to burst from bacteria
haunted with cobweb
a fruitful heart home
roots weaving through
mushroom networks
another rotting log
feeding the forest floor

Cables and Cement – Steve Denehan (he/him)

I remember the fear
blooming to my edges
to the tips of the hairs on my arms

he rarely raised his voice
but the roars came
so loud that when they stopped
the absence of them left me shaking

seventy years ago, now
he had called for us
my brother and I
we ambled into the back garden to find him
collar open, sleeves rolled up
smile wide, eyes squinting in the long sun rays

Time for another lesson boys.
he had taught us how to sharpen a chisel
how to melt lead to make toy soldiers
how to catch a jackdaw
that day was the day we learned to mix
and to lay
cement

we looked at each other
the three of us
smiled
got to it
didn't talk much
but he had a hell of a whistle

and I admired his forearms
tight bunches of cables rippling under tan skin

a small section of the path had emerged
cracked and broken
unwanted magic
from the late winter snow
when we had finished it was new again
perfectly smooth
a job well done
we looked at each other
the three of us
smiled
my hands were caked with concrete
I noticed a cut on my wrist
the blood was stark against the grey
I hadn't even felt it

our cat appeared
we watched in silence
nobody moved
nobody spoke
as he nonchalantly padded across the cement
eight slow motion pawprints
my brother and I turned to our father

seventy years later, I can still see him
his face and eyes a furious red
the veins in his temple
pulsing angry worms
his neck, hard and thick and ready
for roars that came and kept on coming

then there was silence
he threw up his hands and eyes and arms
I heard him mutter
I give up.
and watched him walk away
into the house
into the sitting room
onto his armchair
where he burned
defeated
for the rest of the day

today my brother and I met at the old place
the first time in a while
we stood shoulder to shoulder
looked down
laughed to ourselves
as rainwater filled the pawprints
an empty, concrete day
he is gone, long gone
and we are soon to follow

Yearbook Page 47 – Betsy Merbitz (she/her)

To my high school butch

I'm sorry
for my dripping wet halter top
and denim miniskirt
at the car wash fundraiser
for the arches of my bare feet
balanced on the black rubber tires

Sorry for the school musical
for the day we were building sets together
your shoulders taut, your forearms steady
as you listened to me agonize
over the boy running the lightboard
and tightened your grip on the vibrating drill

I'm sorry for the chocolate chip ice cream cone
I begged you for a taste of
licking my lips
and widening my eyes

Sorry for staring
during the sharp high-notes
of your saxophone solo
as the hollows and pockets of your cheeks
pulsed in and out

Sorry for the hairs standing up
on the back of my neck
as you fumbled with the clasp
on the necklace my latest boyfriend gave me

I'm sorry for couple's skate at the ice rink
for the blade of my skate
playfully spraying snow
at the boy from the rival high school

Sorry for the prom pictures
for the vibrant purple satin
slit up to my thigh
for the blonde soccer player's matching boutonniere

It should have been you in those pictures
wearing a silky black suit
pinning a rose to my smooth-fitting dress

It should have been your tie
I tugged at
to bring your breath
closer to my neck
Your shirt I unbuttoned
on the sagging couch
in my parent's basement

So I
Rewrite those years
of awkward first dates
and clumsy-tongued kisses

Knock that chocolate chip ice cream cone down
and let it melt on the concrete
behind the bleachers
Grab that drill out of your hands

I glide
over to you
during couple's skate
with an outstretched arm
and our cheeks
flush pink

Molting Season – Kael Knoxton Martin (he/they)

It sheds purity   like animal hair, November picking us up by
the neck, offing us one by one; the granted sunlight died with him,
the burning burning itself in the tray with his ashes. The picture
wasn't captured right and the shadow of my father stands in front
of my face, superimposed on top of the heart in my hand. He had
always wanted a boy, a blue patchwork blanket hand-sewn by God
covering my rest, his wish granted in a diner on my sixteenth
birthday, me pouring sugar packets into milkshakes and the blood
clot forming in his body with dried eyes and more hands, latent
fingerprints pressed into hospital chairs. The milkshake was
raspberry and so were his lungs, his skin as grape candy from the
chest up. Shed ashes   like lovers. The worst part is not another
winter corpse, the worst part is that the mistakes had stopped
boiling over the pot, the humanity left hot in the pan. He regretted
it, rot in his folds slowly biting the spark of a bad, bruised Georgia
peach. Houses cannot be unburnt. Bodies cannot be dug up with
love. Sheds leaves, trees   bare in the desert. Here is the picture
on the funeral easel: life doesn't "go on"; it sheds, and the heart of
it continues to pulse.

Grand Canyon State – Kael Knoxton Martin (he/they)

The dream scenario:

the city has bones and lungs and, to our surprise, no hands

to touch with. You hold my hand as we look at the big mountain &

the shadows that the soft clouds make over it—see, here they are soft

instead of sharp. Or they're both, like every pathway

on your body. No, I don't believe in miracles, I know

how to explain it all: why you loved me and why it had to be cut out, why

I never get scared when I'm on the phone with you/when I'm talking to
God/when I'm considering

the smaller, hidden message of the statement;

I'm going to die here, holding hands with the man who ruined my

idea of men. And that's

something we all do in Arizona, until our palms sweat. I say *mama, I wanna
be a real boy,*

but I don't know how to be real, or a boy, or anything

that'll get me into Heaven. I do now. You spend twelve years

afraid of your own stretched-out skin

and get back to me, okay? I take you out

sightseeing; *here is where my grandfather died and here*

is where I broke my arm and here

is my old school building. The dream scenario, of course,

is something I am forced to consume, my head held

down into the bathtub:

I don't exist outside of the scathing

Phoenix sun.

Unfinished Business – Kael Knoxton Martin (he/they)

I wrote to her in the hospital. I want to believe
in the truth I teach to my other selves—
the truth that says I didn't deserve it, the truth that writes the
tragedy
of our entwining paths down in holy, inextricable code—
the truth that absolves me—
but it can't quite stick its emergency landing. This faith
crashes onto its side, the machinery igniting, decimating every
passenger
into charred bits of sacredthings. I can't see myself. I can't
divine my future into something palatable, I can't
whittle my history into an innocent, inanimate figure; my hands
don't work
too well, these days. They tremble over the moonlight and they
envelop me
in space's scratchy fabric, chafing
my skin into a painful, similar red. As such, I can't sculpt anymore.
The raw truth,
severed from everything else, is that I couldn't keep my eyes on my
own paper
or my words quiet during lockdown drills
or my handwriting legible
and so I deserved her wrath.

I still wrote to her
in the hospital. I kept saying it but I don't think
she listened—*in another universe I am writing*
love poetry when I don't notice. In this universe your hair
curls pink around your finger and each strand
cocoons around me in the higher realm. This, of course,

means that I love you. Of course it means
that I love you. In this universe I am writing
about multiple people, and I cannot distinguish between
their faces, each memory drained from the basin. I am still going to
write to all of you
in the hospital. I write to everyone when I'm in the hospital; that's
just how it's always been. My soul
is tethered to the bedframe.

Bowls – Kael Knoxton Martin (he/they)

I like to think that I was raised here, that I'm hiding something big
underneath the rug—a key to a door

inside of my chest, where I keep the hurt locked up

and the men locked up

and force them to lap water out of bowls. We regret to inform you

that your husband is a bad man, that he tried to drown your
daughter

in the kitchen sink. So sorry for your loss,

says the windowsill above, she was dead

before the water, the water only solidifying her status

as "taken too young,"

the escape trickling down her neck

& taking her into the next life, bringing her

to the next family

who will get it right this time

and learn how to love without it all. Without tarnishing. Without
drilling

little holes into her skin

to make her love spill out,

a prisoner's last meal.

I like to think I was raised here,

that one day the rain will rise up

through the window and wash away

the inedible parts of me: the fatty bits,

the too-rough skin, the rotten entrails,

the secrets I hid underneath the rug.

After this, the inconsolable rain puts

the little red pieces of me into a bucket & makes me useful,

makes me holy, uses my body, my discarded

sucked-on bones

to make the plants grow. I was raised here. My

hair grew here, sprouted long

from the water in the kitchen sink

until the abomination underneath

tore it off. Or perhaps

I am hiding a second skin under the rug,

instead of the key. I'm living a double life,

skinning potatoes for the Church potluck

instead of mourning you. You're always tied up in

every memory:

chained like a dog,

handcuffed by the policeman, inside

the torn off pages

that I keep underneath the rug. Some things are better left buried,
says God

to me as I run up and down the hallway. I am eight,

and after that,

with no white spaces

or line breaks

or ghosts to keep the time from passing—

I'm dying, or I'm already dead, or waiting

stuck in the world between life and death

                    living and dying

                    loving and loving

                            and

                    loving,

so it's safe to say that God is the kitchen sink

and we've all forgotten how to pray, the dishes rotting in the
drought.

Untitled – Mykyta Ryzhykh (he/him)

The naturalization of hatred
Every day the giant boulders of the brain create little sons to atone
for guilt
Are sons resurrected?
The magnolia outside the window blooms expressively, quietly, as if
guessing something

Anger-dictatorship
I pretend to be a god every morning over a cup of coffee

Stars-blindness
Castrated calm screams in the language of stones
Motherland of life
The taste of faith
Wrath service of the gun

Stone-ruin
Time to change clothes and pick up picks

*Previously published in *A Thin Slice of Anxiety*

Upstaging Icarus – Grant Shimmin (he/him)

The brown hare of dawn was my walk's rare surprise. Under the mist-crowned hills we met suddenly, the long-legged loper alarmed by the presence of an interloper, turning to bound back up the long-grassed slope, full frightened flight. The protruding ears of its lagging companion swiveled to follow. But as I gazed at the brow of the brown-hared hill, I realised this might be a one-time meeting, and I wasn't ready for it to be over. I wanted to see the hares run with abandon. I closed my eyes, stretched my arms wide and leapt into the air, soaring, careful to keep my shadow from crossing their frantic path. "Don't be afraid, Mr. and Mrs. Hare," I called. "All I want is to see your brown ears bobbing, your long, angular limbs flexing and stretching as you sprint at blinding speed." And as I watched, awed by their athletic ascent, not once did I think of what I could not do.

Tell me about your last joyful wave – Grant Shimmin (he/him)

Rolling in the shallows
At the whim of the intermittent surge
The ribs protruding from the skin
stretched tight across your pliant torso
as clear as my sudden need to know
What made this your last resting place
if indeed your bodily journey ends here?
As you roll, stiff whiskers spear the surface
An eye shut forever is captured in mine
I so want to know your story
But more, I want to ask of the water
holding you: As I enter may it touch me
with a little of the spirit of adventure
you are ceding to these shallows

Cemetery Walk in Winter – LindaAnn LoSchiavo (she/her)

Lorn marble angels greet their unannounced
Guests, stone cold palms displaying dignity
And menace, indicating crypts ahead.

Winds bite our cheeks as snow keeps burying
Our tracks as if the living don't exist.

When alabaster figures seem to move,
We suck in icy January air.

That sky's so white it could wrap up bodies.

        A headstone's cursive warns: "Remember Night!"

Cyber-Toothed – LindaAnn LoSchiavo (she/her)

Crouched behind the flickering light of loneliness, he became data
driven, his right hand red-badged by a wireless mouse. Unable to
roar her to attention in a laundromat or the local dive bar, he
clawed his way in, scrutinizing her browser history, pawing her
passwords, mauling her emails, grooming her apps with malware.

Now anytime she brushes him off in the elevator, pretending to be
hypnotized by her shiny shoes, he can snort-laugh, aware that she
overpaid, that she's being catfished on Hinge, that her vulnerability
is his gateway portal, his kingdom, where his silent strokes rule her
memory disk.

Tomorrow, on her birthday, photographs she thought deleted will
go viral—raw meat to satisfy the bandwidth of his grudge, the
slaughter, smooth and neat.

When a dead battery halts the finale, he's forced to stretch his
haunches while rubbing his eyes, dry and itchy from the screen's
wide savannah. Fur on his neck stiffens as he exhales a tawny dream
of mastery, emptiness caging everything together.

Night gauzes the windows, glamorizing souvenired pizza boxes,
empty six packs, and encrusted plastic food trays stacked like cairns,
waymarks of the dead.

Footprints in the Snow – LindaAnn LoSchiavo (she/her)

It's the same dream. It wakes me up each time.
Could it be some ghost family returned?

Asleep, strange shards of memory poke me
Like spikes. The walls are melancholy now
Since she slipped out that winter, calloused feet
Shoeless although it snowed for hours. Chills
Came creeping into corners by the stove
And stood behind me when I held a knife.

My neighbors said police checked mental wards,
All accident reports, and combed the woods.
They found no trace. Her husband sold the house.

Neglected properties need TLC,
Attract those good at caretaking. It's strange
Quiet arrives in sudden blasts of cold,
Announcing it resists all ownership.

I don't recognize my own fireplace.
Who cut this cord of wood, left embers, ash
Inside the pit? When I bend to smooth sheets,
I sense cool whispering. The window shines,
Reveals it snowed tonight and left fresh prints,
Small, delicate. The person was barefoot.

I am afraid to be responsible,
Afraid to be asked questions. Please, stay away.

Wished Away – LindaAnn LoSchiavo (she/her)

When she sang, leaves escaped her lips, verdant
Jewels, fluttering and dancing through the room.

At first, her parents were struck with wonder.
Oak leaves, then maple, ginkgo, cottonwood
Forced the furniture into pantomimes,
Confused the cutlery, alarmed the rugs.

After two weeks, her parents consulted
A witch who said, "Leave her in the forest."

He aspired to become a nightingale,
Gave his wealth to exchange skin for feathers,
Tuned his voice to chirps, his toes to talons.

A mature hazel tree welcomed them both,
Long endowed with sorcery of its own.

When he trilled, she flung gold leaves at the sky,
Parsing the bones of each note, awaiting
A charm that would change her life, signal love.

A throaty troubadour, his nocturnes wooed
A female bluethroat nightingale. Mating
At midnight, silence partnered their duet.

After tasting such celestial surfeit,
They wove a nest, waited for eggs to come.

There's less magic in pre-dawn's peekaboo
Since nightingale ignores her leaf parade.

She's an old-fashioned roadside attraction,
A spectacle without an audience.
Leafless now, she passes through days like wind.

Types of Emptiness – Devon Neal (he/him)

If you died, people would say sorry,
touch my shoulder in an easy way,
and tell me to take my time.

I would have days off work
and the neighbor would bring be a pecan pie.
Months later if I was staring at nothing,

they would give me time to stare at nothing.
If they saw me out walking
among October leaves crawling on the road,

they would call me brave. I am not brave,
as you know, nor am I off work,
even though the marrow in my bones

rots with loss. This was not a theft,
something silent in the night. When they look
at me, they know this is the type of emptiness

that takes work, and even if I take
my time, I'll only spend it
with empty bones and guilty hands.

The Wound – Devon Neal (he/him)

I forgot in the warm haze of sleep,
the drunk heat of quilt, the deep bells
of the alarm speaking in darkness.
I forgot in the automatic routine
of socks from the drawer, stepping around
the treadmill, lifting up on the bathroom
knob to stifle squeaking. Even in the light,
I forgot as I held my fingertips out
waiting for the kiss of steam-haunted water.
It wasn't until I was in the shower,
lathering clouds of soap into my scalp,
that I found, again, the long wooden shaft
driven into my skull, the tooth-shaped
arrowhead crying poison into the folds
of my brain. If I could go back to sleep
before the morning starts to brighten,
maybe I could forget again.

Celexa – E.N. Loizis (she/her)

You used Celexa like sparklers
on a birthday cake
a flash of light

You're alive!

You were an island
pulling away from land
the lights ahead
turning to flickering dots

as stars do
or joyful moments
when you remove
                              yourself

from them

until all that's left
a splash of mother's milk
across the firmament
of your existence

and how you'd love to crawl
back into her
re-enter the womb
a supernova in reverse

all new brightness
unaware of the vastness
of the dark around
and the lightyears
till the moment you implode

Stardust pain
is a real thing
Oh, the sweetness
of a life

yet unlived

side effects – Simone Astrid (they/any)

drained water bottles in the car. genuflect at glass double doors and
a thermometer to the forehead. mask4mask. sign forms for the
receptionist in my best penmanship. routine maintenance, 3-month
follow-up, 3-month follow-up follow-up. alcohol swab in the crook
of the elbow. a prayer before the needle prick. viscous vials, my
blood in the tray with everyone else's blood, and jesus' blood, too.
grounding breaths in the bathroom. urine cup on the sink, unholy
water. nurses in black scrubs. nurses in back rooms. miracles in
packets and pill bottles and side effect sheets. pull lived side effects,
the hunger, tiredness, like tarot cards.

scrambled. – Simone Astrid (they/any)
CW mentioned (not graphic) suicide, physical/verbal abuse

i wake up anxious
discomfort deep
foreboding like waiting.
dozing on an eggshell bed under
eggshell covers in an eggshell apartment.
i think of you before i sleep—
all claws and elbows.

i remember you with fangs,
foaming at the mouth
must be exaggeration
just flecks of spit.
maybe your teeth were sharp, i can't

remember

that night the car
behind the coach house
the garage the alley
don't feed the rats signs and neighbors' broken
furniture.
taunting. headlights reflected off other cars.
the cold of the bumper's

metal

railings on the fourth of july
i stopped you from jumping off michigan
avenue into the river,

emptied my bank account
for a taxi.
wiped off anger, contempt,
crunched tight between your teeth and
spit into my face,
extra phlegm for good

measure

my tone of voice
to ask where it hurts,
how i can help.
i leave the room bruised.

i peer through cracks in my doors,
no 6 a.m. snarling.
i'm cleaning my house,
changing my sheets,
dusting off eggshells.

the results support the hypothesis – Simone Astrid (they/any)

unstable brain arousal, top-down dysregulation condition, our
multiple regression analysis detected hyperactivity and sensation
seeking. psychiatrists prescribe artificial sensation, make an
appointment for next month. *good luck keeping it with time
blindness, live in the now or not-now.*

smaller structure in prefrontal and anterior cingulate cortex. my
brain is shrinking? *(in the rat model, we're the rats.)* see it predict
sustained attention, cognitive switching, and inhibition issues.
patients using stimulant treatment and their shrunken right
hippocampi nap between doses. caffeine makes me tired.

snap decision. current research suggests impulsivity and impaired
learning are delighted to be positively correlated with dopamine
reuptake. catch the late diagnosis.

THE OTHER IN THE ROOM – John Grey (they/them)

Her bangles are strung with human teeth
Her cameo is an eye in aspic.
She wears a knife tight against her ankle
and a hangman's rope around her waist.

But it's late.
She's all you have for company.
Her nails dig deep into your arm.

She gets right to your otoliths,
twists your senses for her own ends,
Your vision is revoked,
replaced by hers.
That's why your eyes bleed.
And your thoughts are trampled
by her horsemen.

Suddenly, like eels slithering
out of coral caves,
her lips, her tongue,
are coming for you.

A bite-like tingle evokes
your nerves' uneven response to stimulation.
A hiss, a sucking sound,
arouse uneasy rhythms in your heart.

NATURE BOY – John Grey (they/them)

You come from a deeper forest
than the one that quells my footsteps
with its trail of fallen leaves.
That's why, though I feel your presence,
you remain unseen, unheard.

There's nothing you can
actually show me.
There are no words
in your vocabulary.
Yet, with each new step,
I feel as if I belong to you.

Here, by the water,
I peer at my reflection,
and then, and only then,
within the ripple,
there's the hint of a face reflecting
that is not my own.

Father, forest sprite,
demon, or God—
my choice I wonder,
or nature's irrevocable design.

elegy for hope – Audrey Wu (she/her)

you slipped out early this morning

the silk of your nightdress clinging to your femur

you tore your fishnets when your hands were in my hair

and once, when you thought i wasn't looking, you tried on angel
wings from my nightstand

let a laugh ripple from your tongue and land on my lips

i wonder if wisteria could grow in the gap between your two front
teeth

if marigolds would wilt between your thighs

you are a lady who lines her eyes in red

who thinks birthdays and stars are bullshit

who doesn't believe in beauty or doorknobs or

candelabras or love at first sight

and yet, you believe in me.

Warren – Kevin Foote (he/him)

Pre-dawn light glowed along its fur
It didn't dart, nor dash, nor anything near hiding
But hopped beside me
So close to my leg
That my headlamp should've scared it off

For fifty yards or so, we had where we had to run,
The path we shared
Had no space for fear
No signs among the brush, the stones, the grass
That Kevin & the Cottontail needed
To change our course

We ran while rockets hissed over the Gaza Strip
Landing, cruelest of crackling, through Israeli cars
Killing couples
Silencing second dates before they could begin
We ran while moans of mothers rang above Gaza City
Shrieking, fiercest of feeling, over the high rise residency
Laid low in air strikes
Flattening children
Silencing in seconds lessons students would never hear

We ran while orange and yellows slowly grew
Over the edges of the road smattered with stones
Stones small enough for a child to throw at a tank
Before he would hold the gun, hold the RPG,
Hold the brother in his arms one last time
After taking the life of someone else's brother.

We ran without a worry
Of who was the animal
And then we went our separate ways
To our warrens.

The memories that separate us – Alannah Guevara (she/her)

My daddy jolts from nightmare—
a bygone beckoning—
and pushes away the memories
that separate us
to find me, his baby boy,
asleep against our reckoning night
and far from what lies ahead.

My daddy twitches smile;
tastes the salt in our futures.
In his dream I become man,
and his heart does not give at 53
to some unscrupulous night
I cannot forget.

My daddy still dreams
in this memory. We still have time
like the stitching of the blanket,
the barrier between us.
We exist in stillness that night,
and we both still breathe.

Striae – Alannah Guevara (she/her)

Her flesh pulls taut tender memory,
bruised in lush strokes which etch ever deeper
and fade into eggplant scrawlings;
a reminiscence on the waiting days.

Hallowed, drawn deep with deitic design;
the chaos in a natural existence.

She, the mother of all persistence,
she, the empire of dusk;
gambled the soil for seed,
wrought live oak from turmoil,
paid in ounces of coldsweat,
and midwifed the colors of flesh.

The only time I saw my grandma after she died

from complications arising from COVID-19
she was outside of a movie theater
she met me at the entrance with red velvet
garland draped across gold-plated stanchions
erect with discriminate intention to form intestinal queue
useful in the ritualistic act of waiting your turn
as we whispered our hellos
I came to realize that this was the first time
I spoke with my grandma in months and
I felt the sudden urge to apologize and
I felt the impatience of a single misstep and
I felt the heat of a threshold's breath and
I felt the walls slip into windows and
I felt obliged to ask the box office for a moment of privacy
before turning to my grandma to ask
where have you been?
and she said to me what does it matter
if you can't go there yourself?
and I said that's all right with me but
isn't it late now and time to come home?
and she pulled me near with a gentle force
the kind only a mended woman can conjure
and between COPD breaths she purred
I love you but you're on your own
I love you but you're on your own
I love you but you're on your own

– **Alannah Guevara** (she/her)

Intermingled – Alannah Guevara (she/her)

Do you feel my chicharrón muscle
betrays my E. Lee blood? Would my
ancestors explore common ground
and part cumulous religion
just to smite me? Would they realize
then that time is no less than mortal?
In what certain terms did they believe
themselves kings? Biblical, chesslike,
or cluster rat? How do I disentangle ferns
from fishing wire while I am on the hook
and the garden begins where the plantation
ends?

Subject/object – Dorothy Lune (she/her)

of this photo essay: everything about
        it being honest stop me in
my tracks, return to the eleventh shameless
year of age. Jump
        ship, land in

Bermuda—earth spins without looking back,
        it does not want to feel natural.
Floor of her body, like a mossy-grown
tambourine, she plays a tune called
            lacquer-sweet—fend off anything hurled

re-up my stone basket, I'm running
        out soon, it is full.
My muscles grilled by a hot letter opener,
reddened past recognition,
        what is that,

what is it. The editors will love
        this: kneed the area, it
asks for it, pluck clovers
out of my nipples, wrapped
        in glucose film—my areolas

bleed like a revolted bracelet, they ask
        for it. The off-season rate: five bucks
o' shot. Shoot me on
moss & baptize me in benzene,
dry me flat on permission, that
        camera loves me.

The Star – Dorothy Lune (she/her)

Let's say I   discovered the theory of
relativity, I day dreamt,   I kept it down.
I love you I   love you   regardless,
postbellum, October is in your   blood—
my god, you are   made   of straw.
We use   dehydrated   fish to   feed
mammals in the aquarium.

I fed you pails of ice cubes,   in circles
you went,   the ontologists are
skeptics,   mumbles & prescription lens.
I stuck my arm   out,   crawled
inside my   mouth knuckle   first,
I am more disappointed in myself.

The only choice is me   me regardless—
in plain sight   she is patient for me
like verdigris on lady liberty   I'm taken
up by Hecate   with all my gratitude
my sights sharp like a waxing crescent.

Nan's routine forget – Lucy Rumble (she/her)

Nan's gone dark again. Don't know where she is or where she's gone, but she's left her biscuits open in the tin again and the front door swinging in the wind. Nan's gone off the rails again. Cruising down on the 7:15 to Brighton city sights, not knowing that those morning thoughts would soon be left behind. We get the gang together (mum and unc and I) and set out on our weekly trip to find that silly sod. We've got no clue she's in Brighton, mind, that's not her usual haunt. We set out to Marks and Sparks thinking it's *a good shout, she'll be in with the eclairs again, stuffing packets of the things into her overflowing biscuit tins*. But she's not there this time. So we're off again, walking down the promenade and posting old pound coins through the slots of those blue-painted binoculars to scour the sea and sky. No sight of Nan, though. We're worried now and ask the seagulls where she's gone, but they haven't seen her stalking here since squarkin' Tuesday morn. We trudge back late afternoon not knowing where to look, not knowing she'd just be home, sat in her usual spot, pretending with her glassy eyes she'd been there all along.

Nan goes off a lot these days, it's become a cat and mouse. Our ritual of fun each week to find her somewhere in the streets, but this time it seems that she forgot herself a little further off. It's got me worried, this new forget, that she'll break the paths we've known, that Nan will go out dark again and never come back home.

Really Imagined – Robert Pegel (he/him)

Prayerful intention leads to another
dimension where the mind wanders
freely above the wants and worries.
Listen to the children singing their songs.
They feel no pain anymore.
Their actions spark thoughts of redemption
for the ones toiling in oblivion, facing the
earth's warped sense of justice.
Today's problems have slid softly into
the wonder of tomorrow.
Upon arrival, debts and trouble will be
left behind to simmer as smoke chokes
the feeble ghosts left powerless.

Dead People Don't Dream Hamburgers – Koss (they/them)

We were already dead but didn't know it. All three of us lost in the fucking woods. I twirled through the trees like a mama Frisbee, calling to Daria who hadn't eaten, frantic as mother panic, as if she couldn't feed her own pie hole. The trees shook like skeleton bones, and suddenly the vortex dropped me like Dorothy in front of Daria, pale and large-eyed, looking pleased she had worried me by disappearing. Handed her a yellow, paper-wrapped burger, and with disdain she spouted, "You could've done better," as the assembly flopped in her loose arm. I turned to find you, Max, relaxed, smiling, and clueless as I that dead people don't eat hamburgers. You laughed your dead laugh and said you'd teach her some manners. Then the wind snared me from ground, and in the whirling air that was me, I heard "gratitude," over and over. Dead don't eat, Max, but gratitude keeps on going. We all could do better, like she said, I guess.

While I was dreamed and dreaming, Daria walked in her sleep, scratching at your bedroom door, agitated and tearful as warbling pigeons dropped outside your windows.

Previously Published in Eunoia

Conversions: I Appeared in Your Suicide Dream – Koss (they/them)

I tried to spoon you in our sleep
you were curled on the dirty cream floor
like a snail in mist / nil / too far gone to care
I wanted to tell you in your dream
not to leave me / that my breath would also cease
you emerged upright in an ivory bath
paired with a musky, ape-like man
palms hard against the tile surround
you on the short end / him on the long side
leaning, tendons stretched against glazed wall
with your ear pressed hard as a conch
whose echo a kind god might sound
your eyes concave / silent bodies angled awkward
your back a blockade / bone-tub drab
I hovered specter-like
thick-tongued / throat-jammed / mute
marking the distance between / around
with my dull eyes stuck in my head
no baptisms / cleansing / ever-sex in a drained hull
only the past, the future, and the present rowed
a null / your back-to-back hetmare / dreamwitness: paralyzed

a black van parked outside, displaying its tangle of wires
its jaw propped wide open:

*Previously Published in Spillway

Max, Carrie's Mother, [No Wonder] – Koss (they/them)

Max / your death just got even worse / Carrie's Mother arrived at your apartment / she's talking about Jesus and telling everyone what to do / she says she's got a direct line to God and apparently knows

Max / Carrie's Mother texts me Bible verses at 5:00 a.m. / I've hardly slept in days / don't give a shit if the pillows are naughty, Max / I'm overwrought over you / something's wrong with her, I believe

Max / what Carrie's Mother said about me when you talked on the phone / why did you leave your speaker on? / she never met me, but she's got god tangled up in her head / her hair / her throat / and vagina / and you know mine's a God-free zone / and she's a homophobe / something's wrong with Carrie's Mother, Max / surely, you must have known

Max / Carrie's Mother called herself and Mr. Ed We / and I was something Other / not part of the straight girl club / even the horse belongs / she said you never ever loved a woman / I told her you loved seven / something is wrong with Carrie's Mother, Max / whatever her heaven is, let's not go there

Max / you are three days dead with your body on lockdown by cops / your purse / your keys / your things / Carrie's Mother accused me of stealing your allotment keys / this is shit I didn't need / there's something wrong with her

Max / Carrie's Mother's eyes are wild / her hair, tangled ringlets / she gets excited, then angry / laughing and crying / then flinging her arms / no wonder the house burned down

Max / Carrie's Mother is interrogating me about your car / the tires I bought / I didn't tell her why you didn't talk about me / if she were smart, she would know / something's wrong with her, Max / normal people don't act like that / why is she even here?

Max / Carrie's Mother side-dissed our relationship while reenacting sex and passion with her make-believe husband / three times / literally kissing and groping the air / she flung her head back like a drama queen / it made me queasy, Max / something is wrong with her / meanwhile, Mr. Ed made up with King Henry VIII over the phone / as if your suicide were some private agreement between them / yesterday she was going to kill him

Max / what does a 45-year-old virgin know about love? / never mind / you are dead

Max / Carrie's Mother's a smug mother-fucker / like no other Jesus thumper I've met / something's wrong with her Max / I've packed up my bags and am headed to Manchester / King Henry's laid claim to your body / I wonder how his new wife will arrange you in their home / I didn't tell Carrie's Mother what you said about your sleepovers / or why you became estranged / but I did text her "homophobe" / when I got to the hotel / sorry Max / you had to have known / no wonder you burned down the school

*Previously Published in Anti-Heroin Chic

About that time I cried in an MRI machine – Ronita Chattopadhyay
(she/her)

I didn't move
because I was instructed not to.
You have to lie completely still
when they do your MRI.

The tears in my eyes
threatened to spill over
and then they did.
I didn't wipe them off.
Couldn't.
Because—MRI.
And I wondered
if the technicians
looking at their monitors
could see my tears too.

And why was I crying?
Was it because of
that irritatingly loyal back pain
or because I felt stuck
(and not just in the MRI machine)
or for my losses and pain
and that of many, many others
holding a searing communion
in my skin and heart and bones?
This is where
I would have marked
all of the above.

Feral Summer – Navila Nahid (she/her)

scores

webs of petrichor
artery-deep

slipping
Summer's nick
into marrow

and I—
apoptosis
to gnaw,
billow west

knifing
aisles of nimbus

until dolloped
upon cut
dew—a

regime
of hungers

and I
broker
here—*the
weight
of my wild*

The Body – Navila Nahid (she/her)
—After Waran Shire

i

M once said I am
more my eyes
than my face—my glance,
a feast of secrets.
I watched her
watch me
cover the fault lines
of my wrists

sometimes, the earthquake
speaks through
the body

ii

The space between
a fast and a gorge
is a buffet

sometimes, the lacuna
is the body

iii

October scores deep,
notches driven
to bone. M gently cleans
each wound.

sometimes, the body
bleeds years
leftover

iv

I sheathe my fissure
from the sun. M fingers
its edge and says
it's the Mississippi
mighty

sometimes, the body
is the wound
before the
weep

v

Will you always fall fast? M asks.
I say nothing

sometimes, the body
is every heart
but mine

vi

At the funeral, M does not
cry. My coffin inearths
empty.

I was never
the body

My Body – Navila Nahid (she/her)

my body
is sixty percent,
water
and forty percent,
consent
        feather-light
        wings
        allowing hope
        to pull

Jill
after Jack
welcoming
fall
        shatter
        on repeat

bitter swigs
of shame
after love
        and pooled
        spite,
        neat

repetition of
mercy
mercy
mercy
after spiral
        counterpoint to

kill yourself

hand
to lined
cage,
    touching
    heart

hundred
percent,
       pulse

I'm Still Mourning – Devon Webb (she/her)

I'm still mourning; I don't want to see her Instagram stories

I don't want to keep having to remember

& remember

what I lost

sometimes I let things go because I have outgrown them

but she dropped me into the gutter

& I wasn't ready for this absence of a goodbye

sometimes I wonder why & none of it makes sense

sometimes I wish I didn't still halfway love her

sometimes I wish she was ugly & unkind

so I had a reason to be thankful that she left me behind

but some loss isn't victory it's just: loss

some heartache isn't poetic it just. hurts.

some tragedy isn't an opportunity for art it's just

the craft of broken things—like sure you made something of it

but that doesn't make it less broken, less a tragedy

sometimes I wish I could forget but love is easy to remember

sometimes I wish I could smile into the silence but it's so loud

sometimes I wish I didn't care & I pretend but

if you know you're pretending I guess it doesn't count

I wish I could send her a text message about some dumb thing but

that was another age & there's a vacant space where

we used to coexist

& it'll fill back up again, I'm sure, but she won't be here to see it.

Vows – Ambica Gossain (she/her)

I smile the satisfied look
of a party well done.
A son's birthday,
one I was happy
to curate to perfection,
a special request, at his behest.
Eyes dancing the taste of freedom,
after three years of his unvaccinated
sentence to a covid resistant "bunker."
A delicious ambience of buoyant
kids high on sugary sodas,
slicing the sky with bubbles
the size of a tunnel
they could walk through themselves.
And thirsty moms
chugging refillable glasses of champagne.
Relieved to finally celebrate
having the brats off their hands.

It was a social engagement.
I was happy to entertain for a change,
unlike the pretentious pomp I was accustomed
to accessorising my sprawling lawn with.
Covid unleashed a crazy rush of
drop-dead-any-second partying.
The jailbreak from doctors who might
usher guests back behind bars
(or into hospital beds in an ER).

A comeback with a vengeance,
life support (suicide?) of alcohol, sheesha
and cigarettes in place of an oxygen mask.

My husband interrupts my patting
myself on the back
with the week's to do list, a written buzzkill.
Invitations we owe because of the
ones we receive.
The obligatory mop up of vomit
before I regurgitate the drunken mess
of the life I didn't sign up for in my vows.

We argue our sides,
my hands gesticulating protest
against the proliferation of the chaos he thrives in,
the very din I can't hear myself think in.
His anxious feet kick up the dirt
of everything up in the air.

A clock chimes a welcome intermission
of bedtime.
I compartmentalize, tucking the thank you
of my son's smile into bed.
My own temptation to crawl under
the covers with him hung out to dry
with the unfinished conversation to come.

My son's scent lingers, a soothing
procrastination from a return to
the acrid confrontation;

my husband's controlled simmer
about to boil his lid off.
I make the "suggestion" he tape my mouth shut
after his over the shoulder accusation,
me seeking outside help to resolve our differences.
I hope for the sake of no further argument
he's referring to my "no good" friends,
and not to the therapist I'd recently
begun to FaceTime.
(Online, an easier mountain to climb.)
He brusquely demands the key to our home bar
(I refuse to ready) for another onslaught of guests.
Much preferring to dust the surface of things
Or sweep under the rug
(I tripped on straight into the arms of a lover)
rather than contend with the sandstorm
swirling between us.

The Warmth – Sarah Sands Phillips (she/her)

The warmth
             that
leaves
      wet plaster

is the warmth
   I still feel

        between us
never cured.

Lettings – Sarah Sands Phillips (she/her)

The lettings are lined and
drawn with ash and ink

smudged with oil and skin
stared into existence

They take the form of defeat
in their listless flat nothing

Were they just words
that were let go

never taking a day for granted again – Linda M. Crate (she/her)

you were spooked by the blood,
thought it couldn't mean
anything good
when you got a nosebleed
after coughing your lungs out,
spitting out phlegm;

but you remind yourself
that you've always been healthy
and you're not living in a
horror movie

even if life does feel rather like
a dystopia these days—

you remember the warning
on the pills that you mother got
you to deal with the cold
to not take them if you have an
issue with your liver or your thyroid

so you resolve to not take those
pills again;

you don't tell a single soul—

when you wake up in the morning
you promise the gods and goddesses
that you'll never take it for
granted again.

if you lived here you'd be home by now – Taylor Bowman (she/her)

if you lived here   /i'd carve out your loneliness for
oxygen/divest the seeds in us so we can't grow branches like
dead trees/plant myself inside your nervous system to make a
home/i'd make your body an unanswered question/a ball of
light/sever your tongue with my limbs/tap my fingers along
your spinal cord/bring this body of water close/make you
pretty/whisper in your mouth that loneliness is still time spent
with the world/turn bone into land/wander off and get lost/i
would not be good/   you'd be home by now

in the event of my death, read this – Taylor Bowman (she/her)

when the cancer came and didn't leave a survivor   my family
got angry—vengeful, even   as they each collected a piece of
my brother's body   like conquerors—this land is mine
they alienated one another   my mother would not speak to me

and i couldn't understand why   but while they were choking on
their grief,   i could unwrap mine from my body   like my
favorite blanket   fold it up neatly   so you can see all
four corners   and place it back in the closet

selfishly, i thought about my own death   my family again in
turmoil   if i could die quietly i would   i'd cover my body
with soil   lie on the ground until the roots   wrapped
gently around me   and pulled me under

it'd be a mutual agreement   the earth takes back what it already
owns   and i'd be spared from my family's anger   there'd be
no memorial that my mother   could stay home from there'd be
no piece of me anyone could have

my family would blame the earth   in another time when they
need each other   they'd sit in different rooms while in the
same house—frustrated words melting on their tongues like sugar
the earth would just keep spinning   demanding nothing but
everything from them

Every Open Eye – Alex Carrigan (he/him)

Everything I choose to regret
will leave red circles
on my bones.

I feel a trace
underneath my skin,
lines of salt
that build on the cracks.

My veins uncrossed,
exposed my bones to the sun,

and take the weight of
hard thoughts on.

I feel it inside,
shifting down the sides,

diffusing into my breath
and given words to
all the mistakes.

I see a line
taking the regrets
back to nothing,

words I clear from
myself. I believe the trick
of that course would keep

me on the ground, could keep

me still, will leave me
one more breath.

I promised to bury
that weight and cover up

the trace, to wait for
a lifeline out
of the outlines.

Finals Season – Syd M. (they/them)

tick   tick   tick////
     tick   tick   tick////

        trying to write like I am running out of time
           words running across the pages, lapping
           new lines,

tick tick tick////
     tick tick tick////

        pumpkin spice courses through the veins,
        adrenaline rushing,
           the leaves start dancing as the warm wind
           blows,
               trees becoming naked as time goes
               on,

tick tick tick////
     tick tick tick////

        every week, more flashcards with biology
        definitions,
           to be reviewed with precision, passion,
           prowess,

tick   tick   tick////
    tick tick tick////

        the wind blows harder, and crisper, cool to touch,
           sweaters and scarves become the norm,
                uggs and doc martens crunch the
                fallen acorns,

tick tick tick////
    tick tick tick////

        everything must be done before the last leaf falls,
           before the 11:59 deadline posthaste,

tick tick tick////
    tick tick tick////

        finals season is here, every moment matters,
           clutters of notes, annotations and coffee
           stains,
                restless stormy nights have lead up
                to the last exam,

tick tick tick////
    tick tick tick////

        the minutes become hours, the crispy winds blow
        harder,
                it all comes down to my best performance
                versus shivery panic,

tick tick tick////
     tick tick tick////

          frosty flakes pour down, the gusts have calmed, all
is well,
             papers written, questions answered, mental
exhaustion,
               time finally stopped for a moment
to catch a breath,

Lighthouses and Other Things that Remind me of Blood – Adele Evershed (she/her)

When I was booking a get-away for my husband's sixtieth birthday I saw a photo of a lighthouse decorated like a barber's pole. A helter-skelter of red against a cone of white gauze, and isn't that what they say about a barber's pole—blood and bandages? Though it always makes me think of losing my virginity.

He—my husband—likes lighthouses, you see, although he is scared of heights, so we visit and venture up every forlorn tower we happen upon as if we are caught in a Kafkaesque reality TV challenge to climb every bloody lighthouse in New England.

Once inside the spiraling stairs, like our ancient quarrels, go round and round before doubling back on ourselves. And my husband clings to the walls and his old excuses and I rush on hoping the things behind us will grow smaller from a higher vantage point. On the last day of the season we arrive at Little River Lighthouse. The island is full of indifferent gulls and catholic cormorants preaching from the rocks as the fog bell chimes relentlessly like cholesterol in my blood. At the back of my throat the sting of seaweed sits like a death haiku I can't find the words to finish—maybe because that sixtieth milestone is just around the bend for me too. I'm brought out of my reverie when my husband kisses me, he smiles humming along with the tide and then he says I'm going to stop shaving—let my beard grow as unruly as the sea. And he retreats into the candy colored cottage. I sit and stare at the granite water as the cormorants lecture me about old betrayals and force me to drink in the dampness. Suddenly a painted lady lands on my arm, she flaps around like a halfhearted apology then disappears into the mist. And I feel like chasing after her but instead I fit my feet into the footprints left in the dewy grass and follow my husband inside.

scenic road
we navigate the twists
of a long marriage

Stress Fractures – Adele Evershed (she/her)

In the raw clay—I coiled and pinched and tipped you back—a boneless
creature—hand built denied the dynamics of throwing
I was in control of our shape but I knew my handle could never hold
the weight of us—the join would never last in the fire
So I heaped it with blood and fish and bones—shadowing with ferns to
fume and give you color—staying with my precious work all night
I marveled as I juggled it from the pit like a game I had won
The line was barely there sealing our halves together in a jar as full as
the moon

You liked to stretch the world between your fingers—
I built in solid sections to the sound of drums—my heart so loud—
gobbing them out
To pass the time you pulled stems and leaves but I fashioned worry
beads
The shadows you made laced the floor in flighty patterns—their sound
mimicked violins to make the moon wobble
So I trimmed and turned and cut out the surplus to restore the
balance—offering you a votive of sensible choices
I was never slapdash—
The line was always there—the top wider than the base threatening
collapse

Older you peeled away patterns to reach your shadow—knowing how
to be in the world—
Never wanting to know the darkest part of me I played radio dramas
for company—blame my milky white culture—it built the bones of me
You floated away in a lunar arc—shouting—even dogs in the street
know how to take energy from a crowd
I always knew the bodies that made you should not oppress you and so
I'd left air pockets for you to breath
You never understood—my body could not travel beyond my own front
door but my heart always left with you
The line was always there and what remains is a ghost moon of
porcelain sitting on my shelf

Watching from Above China Town – Adele Evershed (she/her)

A police car's high chirping disturbs the air, a poor imitation of bird song in spring. Yet this place is stuck in a forever winter. The one legged man promenades, his black and yellow trainer wasping the sidewalk as a cipher of a girl, thin as a thread, folds and refolds pajama bottoms in a parody of my mother every Monday. I look out from the hospital window as ash flies into the air—a brutal glowing of May blossoms. The maybe people rise and bubble like yeast. Then just as I feel hopeless, a grizzled seagull calls—shabu shabu and those with nothing throw him crumbs. I exchange a long look with the graffitied Japanese fish on the restaurant wall and then we both watch as the world crosses the street as if they are dodging dog doo-doo.

sweater weather
my mother's hair
starts to fall out...

You Once Told Me that Noble Rot Stuck to Me like Shame – Adele Evershed (she/her)

I get the tattoo of our old love burnt off my skin / and I feel raw and vulnerable / like a doe before dusk / I offered my seagulls crumbs so they would not spill my secrets / yet they squawked disunion into the air / and it spread like a rumor / through the village of us

We changed into an industrial landscape / grinding out quarrels / and spitting out ash / so I stole the lyrics of a song / and put them in a poem for you / it felt like a purge / or as if I was trying to resurrect a me / from long ago / when I still believed

Still all those old rotten words had rooted in the core of me / you know the ones / slut and skank and whore / and when you dug them up / I turned into a wasteland /
and then you left with the rain

Now I know there is no nobility in rot / instead it's just a black blanket / that smothers from the inside out / what if I throw it off / and plant daffodils in all my cracks / use those words as manure / then maybe I'll be able to bloom

Well – Adele Evershed (she/her)

Unwell / she lives between / the salt and glass / a ghost crab /
scuttling away from the currents / she doesn't understand

All her long life / she washed shirts / her tears like silver pieces /
thrown into a dry well / where only the ghosts float

And life after life / we recognize the cry / and do nothing / except
feed the water carrier beetles / that left the well empty / in the first
place

They hid our sacred wells / replacing them with ones that gushed oil
/ that were only ever made holy in puddles / with the relics of
rainbows

But now under a hunger moon / we should not waste wishes /
throwing our less than minimum wage / in a well of their making /
hoping to make a splash

We need to take a lesson from the crab / approach them sideways /
so they don't see us coming / and then we'll / snap / snap / snap

FICTION

Baby Dearest – Alison Hallie (they/them)

Twenty days after not our first but our final end, after Cancer season came to a close and the new moon in Leo hung high in the sky like an offering, or a good omen, after I stopped talking about my feelings and started telling jokes again, I dreamt that I held our baby. The very baby I had only seen once before, splayed across the ultrasound screen in black and white a week before we never spoke again. But it was that night, in my sleep, in the endless universe of possibilities of my mind's eye, that impossibly, I met them, held them. I cradled our borne child as if we hadn't already said goodbye.

From the moment my sleep sowed dreams they were in my arms, at peace with me and me with them, their soft, round cheek resting on the upper curve of my right breast while I inspected them. They looked exactly as I imagined they would, healthy in size and skin, with all the soft folds and fat of being well cared for as I tried to discern where my features ended and yours began on their still, well-fed face. Their eyes were closed, surely with dreams of milk and a mother who was still loved by their father, so there was no way to know which of our irises they inherited. Nonetheless they were beautiful, perfect even, the way a baby created of one's own body can only be, so it didn't matter to me that they were also yours because in my arms, warm and real, they were only mine. And I wanted to whisper into their pretty little ears, like perfect seashells, how glad I was to finally meet them, but instead, I caught my breath between my throat and my molars. Too afraid to break our burgeoning bond with words.

So, swaying them gently, I decided that soundless space was our love language "for now," softly sung songs and saccharine speech could come later—we had time for that. We had a lifetime together for them to know the nuances of my slight vocal fry and for me to know the exact octave ranges of their cries, but in that moment, I knew we were best to know each other first in the absolute sweetness of that shared silence. As I held my breath, they rested with my hand on the back of their head. As I felt the gentle pulse of their forming brain beneath my fingertips, I realized that I was already in love, already ready to die for them, already afraid they would disappear if I looked away from them for even a moment. So, I held them closer to my heart, so they would *know*, when their little left hand raised to cup my collarbone, embracing me back.

Somehow it occurred to me that I needed to know their scent. So, impulsively, I lowered the tip of my nose to their forehead to find that there were not the various sweet, scented powders of infancy but your cologne. Although, our child didn't smell like you and your skin wearing your cologne but rather like your cologne on my pillowcase in the morning, your cologne on that thin brown sweater you borrowed from me all winter, or your cologne on me and my skin at the end of the day. I hadn't been allowing myself to miss you during the daylight, but then, in that moment, I was overcome by a sentimentality that I betrayed. I stayed smelling our child, smelling us, smelling what had faded from my sheets, sweater, and self, and I would have done that forever if sleep allowed me, but the boy next to me in the bed I slept stirred. My eyes twitched in discomfort and opened before I could cling to my child closer.

They disappeared from my sight, from my embrace and they were replaced by reality, replaced in my open eyes' vision by a postcard plastered wall, lit by what could barely be called morning. Panic overcame me. I was not ready. I hugged my arms to myself, hard, feeling and knowing exactly how empty they really were. How empty they had been. I looked behind me at the beautiful rebound in my bed and gave myself a beat to nearly hate his handsome face before squeezing my eyes shut. I tried to reimagine our child long enough to give them a name, to kiss them, to watch them grow, but behind my eyelids I only envisioned the blind, blank black of a total lack of recollection.

And there it was again—the grief. I tried not to cry about the loss after loss and yet another reminder of the end after the end, but my stomach felt flat beneath my hands. I couldn't stop my breath from hitching and my shoulders from shaking as I mourned everything, all of it all over again, until I inadvertently woke the naked coke-hungover man next to me.

To my disturbances, he pressed his chest and his morning-hardened penis to me, as he lazily threw an arm over me. When he felt that I did not relax back to dreams, he put his lips to my salty cheek and asked, "Baby, what's wrong?"

Tale of the Floorboards – Sean Robinson (he/him)

The floor above me is creaking. It's the back and forth of my mother. I don't remember her voice, but the whine of the floorboards is a language of its own. I imagine she is making dinner, or breakfast. It is dark, the only light is coming off the boiler—a little glimmer that makes the cellar darker instead of brighter.

But there is work for me to do, the bags do not sort themselves. There is seaming to be done, and patterning, and stitching. Always stitching. There are bags and bags in the dark cramped space of the cellar. If I am not careful, and dutiful, the bags will overflow and I will not be fed.

I do not remember the last time I spoke to anyone but myself. Or heard voices other than the creak of the floor boards. I know that yesterday was darning day, filled with jeans to mend and shirts with rips. They are folded at the top of the stairs and I will not see who takes them.

Today is stitching day. I will take the scraps I've cut and make something in the dark. I am not sure what, but I have three needles left and if I am careful, I can pick thread free from the rag bag. And then I'll sleep, because it is dark, because I am tired and no matter how bad I've been, I will not give up my sewing.

I pull the plastic bags closer to me, making a nest, and begin to look. My fingers find corduroy and denim, cotton, and polyester.

"I wish I could see," I say softly. If I speak too loud, mother can hear me. Or he will hear me. He can't hear me. I can't let him hear me, I can't…can't…

There was the slap to my face and hands on my arms. Pulling at me. Pushing me. There is pain and—I am ripped like a fancy party dress. I am tulle and ribbons and pretty spangles and then there is darkness and the cellar and the bags filled with clothes that I am not allowed to wear. And it hurts and if I am going to play with needles and thread and fabric, I will be punished.

My fingertips cross something in the bag that is different. It's firmer and softer. Lace. I pull it free, and search the bag-nest with my other hand. The seam-ripper has a soft handle, it fits in my palm. I run my thumb across the lace and find where the seam is. In the dark, I carefully cut the thread and carefully work the stitches free.

When it is done, my mother is no longer walking upstairs. There is another set of feet, heavier, and the floorboards scream. I would scream too if I dared. But I pull the bags closer, letting the laundry spill free until I am covered by shirts and plastic.

The door rattles. Once. Twice. And the floorboards whisper that he is gone.

It is a long time before I push free of my hiding place. I have lost the piece of lace, but not the seam ripper. That is still in my sweat-soaked hand. I have never moved far from it since coming to the cellar. Since forgetting what voices sound like, the feel of sunlight. I am tired.

I test the edge of the seam ripper with the pad of my thumb. It is sharp enough, I think. If I committed to it.

"But that's the problem," I whisper. I want to unstitch my wrists and leave the cellar behind. "Commit."

Gramma is sitting on the stairs, beside a bag of laundry waiting to be gone through. She wears a pink sundress with fat roses in the print and holds a straw hat in her hands. Her bare feet rest on the floor.

"I'm sorry I never made you anything, Hyacinth," Gramma says, as though she has not been dead for ten years. As if I weren't being punished for liking things that I shouldn't like, as if I weren't trapped in a cellar with bags piled high.

"What did you say?" I ask.

"I'm sorry," she says again, running the rim of her hat between her hands. "I'm such a terrible grandmother. You know, the job doesn't come with directions. So I just fumbled along. I'm sorry."

"No. No. What did you call me?" I say, pushing the bags aside.

"Hyacinth," she says again. As though it were the name my mother called me. "It's your name, isn't it?"

"Yes," I say, wanting to cry. "Yes it is."

Gramma smiles and stands, "And today is stitching day, isn't it?"

"Yes."

She sets her hat on the stairs and begins to move through the bags. "I would like to make you something. But what can we make?"

"I don't need anything, Gramma."

In the flickering of the furnace light I can't quite make out the color of her eyes. "You need a lot of things, love. And this is something I can do for you."

She pulls two pieces of clothing free and then kneels on the bags, pushing them toward my face, "These will be perfect, Hyacinth! Absolutely perfect. I know just what we'll make. They'll be the most beautiful purple!"

In her left hand she holds a pair of overalls. In her right is a t-shirt that had been mine once. I can almost make out the words on it.

"Gramma," I say, "Those...those aren't purple."

"But they want to be," she says. "Haven't you ever wanted to be something other than what you were?"

Yes. I think. And I had woken up in the cellar when my mother caught me with her second-hand dress and stockings. If I wanted to be a...a...if I wanted to be bad I would be punished.

"Come on then, get your seam ripper and let's get to work!" We work in the darkness. Gramma singing or pulling bits and pieces from the piles. I rip and sew and try my best to pretend that it is real. That there is someone who knows I am down in the cellar, someone that doesn't speak the language of the floorboards. But I am tired and hungry.

"I need to sleep, Gramma," I tell her. "I don't feel good."

"Just a little bit longer, love," she says. "We're almost done and then you will look so beautiful!"

I had wanted to be beautiful. I had wanted to be many things, and none of the things I had wanted to be could live in the cellar while he and my mother walked upstairs and sent down bags of laundry for me to fix. If I had wanted to sew and play dress up, then I could do it where they wouldn't have to see me do it. Where no one would see me.

My stomach cramps. I do not feel well. I'm tired.

"Gramma?" I say.

"Right here. Just a little longer."

"I want to go to sleep."

"But you can't yet, Hyacinth. We're not done. What are we making, anyway? It can be anything you want it to be. A frock or a jumper. Trousers or a blouse? Anything you want."

There is noise again upstairs. It is loud and heavy. Mother is there and so is he. They are fighting.

"He's coming," I say. There is nowhere to go, nowhere to hide in the cellar with its bags and its clothes and the weak light of the furnace. The floorboards scream that he's coming. The panic is up on my tongue, sitting on it like an angry cat. I want to be sick.

"Ain't no one coming, Hyacinth," Gramma says. "Least of all that man." She stands, wiping her hands down her pink dress. "You keep on sewing."

But I cling to her.

"No. No Gramma, please don't leave me. He'll…he'll—
again…again." My voice rips like a seam. Like my dress, the only
dress I'd ever worn.

I can't let it happen again. "He'll kill you Gramma. Please."

"He won't be killing no one."

And then she is gone and I am left. I am left with bits and
pieces and half-sewn hems.

"Gramma?" I say. But she does not answer. The floorboards
above me are screaming. He is coming and he will…he will.

I start to scream because the door is shaking. The door that
locks from the outside, the one that I am not allowed to touch,
because I will be dead if I do. He tries it again, and again. There is a
louder sound and the floorboards howl with his weight. The door is
beaten, beaten like me. Just like me. And it swings open.

The seam ripper is lost in the clothes and the plastic. I
scramble to find it as the light from upstairs breaks the darkness. It
is so much light that it hurts. I try to find the handle and the sharp
edge, something, to keep me safe. But I can't find it. I can't find it.

Footsteps echo down the stairs.

He is here.

"Gramma?" I whisper, begging. But she is gone. She has
never been here.

"Dear God," a voice says and then coughs. It is not his voice.
It is different.

"Is anyone down here?" the voice says again. I can't help it.
I huddle, pulling the plastic bags up near me. I try to put them
between me and whoever is coming down the stairs.

The figure is backlit by the light from the stairs. I watch as
they trip on the hat that Gramma left on the steps. "Is anyone down
here? Jesus Christ."

He sees me, buried to my neck in the piles of clothes that
litter the basement. So many of them they have formed hills and

mountains, leaning against the boiler, only a small place, where the light comes through is visible. And it smells. There is no way to hide how bad it smells.

"What's your name?" he asks as he crouches.

"Hyacinth," I whisper. Because it is my name. The one my Gramma called me in the darkness. The one that took me into the cellar and the clothes. The one I will never give up to the creaking floorboards or my mother or him. "Did you come to save me?"

"Let's see if we can't get you cleaned up, huh?" he says. His voice is soft.

I grab for what we've been working on. His hands are gentle on my too-thin arms. My clothes hang off me. It hurts to stand. I don't know how long I've been sitting in the dark. I don't remember the last time I ate or when I had something to drink. I feel like fabric stretched too thin. Like my seams are about to rip

"It's my gown," I say, pulling it to me, though he does not ask. "My gramma made it for me."

"It's beautiful," he says, and guides me to the stairs.

The Locust and the Lake – Jeff Presto (he/him)

They haven't told us anything about the aircraft downed over Lake Erie, yet.

I'm not really surprised. We still don't even know why we're being held here.

It's been four days since they moved us here. Me and the rest of the town have all been forced from our homes and relocated to the various gymnasiums of the local high schools and elementary schools without any warning or formal explanation. Rows of cots line the basketball court and a mountain of blankets lies strewn across the bleachers. I'm not sure how many people are being held at the high school with me, but there are at least a couple hundred of us—maybe even three. The crowded hallways make it feel like there might be even more than that, and that's without factoring in the number of military personnel present on campus.

This is one thing that no one ever talks about in the movies or TV shows when a mysterious aircraft gets downed outside of your hometown—aliens or not, if the government takes any interest in what is happening, you'll still end up getting abducted either way.

I was on East 18th Street when it happened. The sky was a blend of charcoal and dark blue, devouring the evening sun overhead as I hurried through the city streets to make it home for dinner. My mother always screams at me whenever I stay out too late on school nights, so I left Reid's house a few minutes earlier than usual to try and make her happy. Reid's house wasn't very far away—maybe a twenty-minute walk if the buses weren't running—but it didn't matter. I was alone when the streets filled up with black cars, and at that point, there was nothing I could do.

They came in from every direction. Military personnel blocked off entire intersections as they herded everyone in sight into oversized trailers attached to the backs of large service trucks. From across the street, I watched as weapons were drawn on those who resisted. Several deafening booms erupted as people screamed and mechanisms fired, but even amongst the chaos, no one got away. I still have a bruise on my forearm from where the arresting officer grabbed me and dragged me into custody. Sometimes I think about what might have happened if I tried to run, but even if I had made it home and avoided being picked up on East 18th, there wouldn't have been anyone there waiting for me. The military swept the town from the west, and my family would have already been forced into the back of a truck. Ending up in a camp, here or elsewhere, was basically inevitable.

I haven't been back outside since. None of us have.

If I still had my cell phone, I'd call my parents and let them know that I was at the high school. My pockets feel empty without it. Cell phones and electronics were some of the first things that were confiscated from us upon arrival. From what I've heard, it is likely that my family is at one of the elementary schools or the community rec center, but I have no way to verify that information. All I know is that they aren't here with me. Hopefully, for their sake, they all ended up in the same place.

Regardless, I doubt they'd sleep any better at night if they knew I was here. I've barely been sleeping at all. Each night that I've spent here has consisted of me staring helplessly up at the gymnasium ceiling. It's the only thing that I can look at that won't stare back at me. Every other direction invites a swarm of watchful eyes that feast upon my curiosity. Patrolmen. Frightened children. Desperate detainees. There's no place to hide from any of it. We're all under constant surveillance and are treated like specimens rather than citizens. All forms of privacy have disappeared.

The entire situation is enough to make my head spin, but there's something else I've noticed about being here that's far worse than any breach of privacy. In the middle of the night, when most people have fallen asleep, a faint sound can be heard coming out of the ceiling ducts. I can remember the sound that a locust makes from the summers that I spent at camp, and this isn't too far off from that, but that still isn't quite right. This noise has range. It pulses with emotions that are far too complex for insects. The noise is difficult to discern, but if I concentrate hard enough, it almost sounds human. This wailing lasts for several minutes each night before it comes to an end, and the high school falls silent until dawn. I'm terrified of what the noise could be, but it isn't coming from inside the gymnasium. If it were, the patrolmen would have put a stop to it. Instead, they simply tolerate it. This observation tells me all I need to know.

There is something else inside the building that they're not telling us about.

I think about this noise constantly. The wailing. None of the other detainees claim to have any recollection of the sound each night. Some of them swear that what I'm hearing is just poor ventilation, while others just stare at me suspiciously. I don't dare ask any of the patrolmen, but I'm sure that they'd give me a similar response. I don't want to ask them anything that will draw attention to myself. I just want to leave.

This is the one thing that me and the others can all agree on, and not everyone here is subtle when it comes to showcasing their anger. Some of the people here are beginning to break down. One man, sporting a long mane of dirty black hair and positioned three cots down from me, is constantly twitching and has started talking to himself. Another man, first row in the center of the bleachers, aggressively guards over his family and yells at anyone who so much as makes eye contact with them. A woman who looks to be in her mid-thirties, her cot positioned beneath the basketball hoop nearest me, is constantly screaming at the patrolmen and claiming that they're taking pictures of her while she sleeps. Nothing about this situation is healthy. We're just expected to do as we're told—and we're told often.

The sudden blare of an airhorn cuts sharply through the room as patrolmen enter the gymnasium from both entrances. They quickly call for our attention and begin to divide us up into small groups. This happens several times per day, and while I know I'm about to be shipped off to a classroom for questioning, the process never gets any easier. We're interrogated on things that we cannot explain and fed information that the military claims to be true. When the patrolman waves me out into the hall, I don't resist. I follow the dozen or so people in front of me as we're transported to a small classroom along the east wing of the building.

As we walk, the whispers and theories grow louder and wilder. I've heard just about every theory surrounding the downed aircraft. That's the real reason we're all here, so all questions inevitably lead back to whatever flew over us a few nights ago. No one will even confirm what exactly it was. Whether it was—a plane, helicopter, satellite, or drone—remains a mystery. The most common theories are that it's some kind of Russian or Chinese plane, but recently I've heard a couple of detainees claim it was a UFO just to fuck with patrolmen. Whatever it was, no one in here has any idea.

I doubt the aircraft was a plane from a foreign country. It's certainly the most plausible explanation, but I'm sure a violation of international airspace wouldn't warrant the shutdown of an entire town. There must be more to it than that. Several patrolmen have claimed that both the American and Canadian shores of Lake Erie have been locked down. If they're to be believed and the military is really occupying the lake, then this is much larger than some failed act of espionage. If it were that simple, soldiers wouldn't be detaining civilians for information. They'd all be out on some manhunt instead.

Unless, of course, they've already found the people they're interested in.

The military must think that some of us either witnessed or were exposed to something. To what, no one seems to know. We just follow orders like obedient lab mice. We go where we're told and we interact in ways that won't get us hurt. The walls inside the high school seem to shrink with every passing day, and the officers wield this power like a tourniquet.

They're waiting for us to break.

We reach the classroom to which our group has been assigned and are instructed to take a seat among the rows of desks. Two officers are already inside the room and waiting for us. They stand in front of a large chalkboard and remain silent until everyone is seated. Their navy-blue suits are ironed and crisp, while many of us have been wearing the same clothes for days. The more decorated of the two officers remains in the center of the room, pins glinting under the fluorescents, while the other moves towards the far end of the chalkboard.

A third officer enters the room from behind us and stands between the seating area and the door. The three men briefly observe the room and watch as a few of us exchange nervous glances. Some of the other detainees choose not to acknowledge the officers. Instead, they sit next to the large set of windows positioned along the opposite wall of the classroom and stare outside at the world that they once knew. It's not much of a view, but it's the only time that we're able to see the sun. Sometimes we can't even see that.

The thought of a closed glass window functioning as some sort of reward is truly pathetic. It makes no difference to me as to which part of the room I'm confined. It won't change our situation. I choose to remain seated next to the door leading back out into the hallway.

"We know that none of you are happy about any of this," the heavily pinned officer says. "But our hope is to not keep you here for much longer. However, for that to happen, we still need your help. We need—"

"We don't know anything," the twitchy black-haired man blurts out from the front row. "What about that don't you understand?"

The room falls silent as the man grows visibly irate. His hands ball up into tight little fists as he slams them down repeatedly atop his desk. He's more unhinged than I've ever seen him in the gymnasium, but any those of us forced to camp next to him could have predicted he'd be among the first to snap. Our eyes bounce between the officers and the man who interrupted them, but nobody moves. The lead officer pauses and gives the man a long stare before he continues.

"What we need from you is—"

"What do you want us to say?" the same man purposefully interrupts, rising to his feet. "We've been stuck inside this building this entire time. With you! We can't go home. We don't know what's going on. We can barely see the sky from in here!"

"Sit back down," the lead officer commands.

"Fuck you," the man barks defiantly. "We're all getting out of here!"

The officers barely have time to react as the man picks up his desk and hurls it at the windows. A loud clang echoes through the room as the desk bounces off the plate glass and causes it to fracture. The other detainees gasp and dive out of the way as the desk ricochets back towards them. The black-haired man quickly loses his balance as his momentum carries him down to the floor. I watch as he lands on his stomach and quickly tries to scramble his way towards the back of the room, but he doesn't get very far. The three officers converge on him immediately.

The officer nearest me has moved away from the doorway and in towards the center of the room. His attention, as well as everyone else's, has shifted onto the black-haired man who has been tackled and pinned to the floor. Thin streams of blood now flow from his mouth and his nose. He's failed to start a riot or spark any additional dissent, but he has created a distraction.

My opportunity to leave is now.

I slide towards the edge of my seat and slowly stand up from my desk. No one turns around as I ease myself away from the scene and open the classroom door. I don't even open it the entire way—just enough for me to slink out. My heart pounds frantically as I enter the hallway. The officers will notice that I'm gone in a matter of seconds, and they'll come looking for me. There's no more time to waste; only to run.

I rush down the hallway, leaving the classroom and the gym behind. My only concerns are reaching the outer wing of the building and searching for any possible exit. There will be more men guarding the perimeter, but I've already made my choice. Even if I'm caught, I just want answers. I can't blindly go back to that gym and spend another night listening to that mysterious wailing. If there really is a threat so large that it requires the town to be forced into involuntary isolation, we deserve an explanation.

A combination of grunts and broken sentences ring out in the distance. I glance over my shoulder and see that the patrolmen, distracted by the commotion in the classroom, haven't made their way into the hall yet. The next few seconds are the most important in my entire life. They're the only thing dictating how much freedom I still possess. I spot another classroom door ahead of me to my left, and veer towards it. The door opens effortlessly and I dart inside. My eyes bounce frantically around the empty classroom as the footsteps in the hallway grow louder.

A large window is positioned along the opposite wall and casts a small amount of light into the darkened room. I rush towards it until I take notice of the thing sitting in front of the chalkboard. The sight stops me where I stand. An empty steel cage, not unlike something that a large dog would be housed inside of at a kennel, is positioned behind the teacher's desk. A white blanket lines the bottom of the cage and hosts a small collection of items. Empty food wrappers, broken zip ties, and a small tennis shoe lay inside. It's difficult for me to imagine someone being forced to live in here, and given the size of the shoe, that person would likely have been a child. I shake my head in disgust and tell myself that the dark splotches covering the blanket are only shadows.

Directly above the cage is something equally alarming. Heavy chalk lines have been frantically etched across the board to form a distressed illustration. I squint and take a step backwards as my mind processes what's in front of me. The drawing on the board is complex but confusing. It depicts a large mass of clouds hovering over the lake shore, with a heavy, dark circle etched into the middle of them. Whether it represents the sun, an explosion, or a portal is unclear. Perhaps the individual trapped inside the cage was unsure as well.

What shocks me most, however, is that there's a wall vent located just above the cage between the top of the chalkboard and the ceiling. It wouldn't surprise me if this ventilation shaft connected to the ductwork in the gymnasium.

My stomach drops as I realize what the noise that I've been hearing every night has been.

I pull open the drawer on the nearside of the teacher's desk and rummage around for something sharp or heavy. The footsteps outside are getting louder, and I'm running out of time. I wrap my hand over a pair of scissors handles and crouch down beneath the desk. When the door opens, I'll be ready.

If there's anyone left inside the gym, I hope they'll be able to hear me.

Soon, the locusts will wail again.

Phantom – Christina Rosso (she/they)

Before it happened to me, I heard stories of phantom limb syndrome. Soldiers feeling excruciating pain where an appendage once existed.

My uncle's left leg was blown off in the Vietnam War, leaving a stump just above where his knee used to be. He never complained about his loss or even mentioned it. Yet I could see the way his prosthetic pinched the skin of the stump with each step, how he took a sharp breath in, the air whistling through the small gap between teeth and lip. One patch of lip remained chapped, always, from the portion of flesh he bit into.

I don't know if he experienced phantom limb pain. I just know he always seemed to be in the midst of a tug of war, the past and present at battle, his movements limited and challenged. A man shackled to his loss and how it didn't fit into the world in which he lingered.

Once he came to visit us in the summer. Back then we lived in the house on Roselawn Lane with the rectangular, inground pool. My siblings and I felt like princes and princesses with such luxury. We took turns diving and flipping into the chlorinated water, rating our gracefulness and the height of our splashes.

"What about a contest to see who can hold their breath underwater the longest?" my uncle said.

I hadn't noticed him get in. I knew it was rude to stare but I couldn't help it. I don't remember ever seeing my uncle without his prosthetic before then. The water distorted the stump in its blue-green ripples. I wondered if he felt an emptiness there, in the space between skin and pool. I wondered if it was something you could ever get used to—a part of yourself disappearing like that.

The stump squirmed as my uncle swam from one end of the pool to the other, his right leg moving like a flipper beside it. He beat all of our attempts at holding our breath the longest.

When it started happening to me, it wasn't like the stories I'd heard about soldiers. I didn't bite into my lip to quell the discomfort. There was no pain, no pinching. Instead, it was a dull tingling, as though my body only offered the numbness as an afterthought.

There was no explosion or accident. I wasn't even afforded the shock of waking up one morning to find the missing parts of myself. Instead one day, in the middle of a perfectly ordinary day, my right hand buzzed, the sensation starting at my knuckles and rushing down the bones and muscles of my fingers to my palm, a tidal wave of paralysis. The numbness lapped at my wrist, my elbow, my shoulder bone. I looked at my arm quizzically, as though that would provide the answer. The appendage was changed, no longer wrapped in freckled skin swarmed with blue veins. It was ghostlike, a luminous undefinable shape.

The next week the buzzing returned, this time nipping at my left toes, traveling to my hip bone. I lifted my pant leg to find that part of my body disappeared, a hemisphere missing from the map I once was able to trace by memory.

By the end of the month, my entire right side was transparent, except for my ear. The shadows of near dusk crept into my bedroom through the windows. I stood in front of the floor-length mirror examining my reflection. The faint lines of bone and dots of flesh that remained of my vanishing map. Half of a face, two ears, half of a torso, one arm. Pale wisps furled in the air, phantasmal ribbons. In the twilight, I fit just so. I wondered how long it would be until I was no longer solid or seen, reduced to swirls of spectral smoke. Until I was an echo, a phantom bride.

My mind drifted to that summer at our house with the inground pool. My uncle holding his breath for three whole minutes, his stump shimmying in the blue-green water as he went from one length of the pool to the next. When he surfaced, beads of water on his forehead and cheeks, he inhaled deeply, replenishing his lungs. Then he grinned at my siblings and me. He walked out of the water then, each step relaxed and effortless. For that moment, he was exactly where he was supposed to be, the battle temporarily suspended. It was the most free I ever saw him.

I took a deep breath and grinned at my transformation in the mirror as the wisps of my former self twirled into vapor.

Hardboiled – Charlie Wührer (she/her)

I say, The parallel universe is laid over the normal universe like tracing paper over a grave, in preparation for a little grave rubbing.

Right. You rub your temples.

It's hard to describe, I say, frustrated. Who doesn't love a good analogy? I give up trying.

Graveyards are for Sundays. The last time I see you, it is a Sunday, and I've given you the sharpest knife in the world.

It's good for tomatoes, I say. Now goodbye.

Wow, you say. It's very sharp. You stroke the blade regretfully. Anyway, you say, goodbye. See you in a month.

Your other girlfriend is unhappy, none of us are particularly happy. We think a month might reset us. You continue to finger the knife. I eat the last avocado slice with my fingers.

Don't let it rust, I warn. Don't let it fester in the sink. Goodbye.

Sometimes, when you've been about to leave, I say I wish I could eat you. I want you inside me, but also my life would be more peaceful with you gone.

But then it'd be over, you say when I say that.

You're holding the knife, the handle is pleasing. The dark unvarnished wood will become water-logged. I want to touch your abs. Something like the magic porridge pot would both hold us and manifest infinite amounts of ourselves to be eaten by each other forever. And who wants peace, is that what we'll think back on?

What will you do now, I say to stall for time as I think about how best to eat you. I've run out of gifts to give.

I'll go to the graveyard, you say. I'll sit on a bench and hold my knife present and cry.

We shake ourselves and pull on our coats. I still want to touch your abs, but they are further away now. Despite a forecast of rain, I ambitiously slip my sunglasses into my pocket.

I'll buy yoghurt, I think rousingly once outside, and cheap supermarket flowers. I will buy a grapefruit. I will open egg cartons and wiggle each individual egg to see if it is stuck to the carton. If I find one that is stuck, I will push it further into the carton until there is a loud crack and I see the egg yolk oozing up around the shell, and then I will wiggle the egg shell again and it will move, lubricated by the yolk. I will close the carton. The insides of the broken egg will dry and stick the egg shell to the carton again. The next person who opens the carton and wiggles the egg will see it is stuck to the carton, and they will not buy the carton of eggs. Nothing soothes me more than a trip to the supermarket.

We say goodbye for the last time, and I think it's pretty boring actually, to keep saying it. I sweep away jauntily. Probably I am in shock. When I turn back and see you leaning against a lamppost, I do not turn into a pillar of salt.

A month is not so long, a friend says. It's negligible in the grand scheme of marriage. Who's talking about marriage, I say, disgusted.

*

In some cultures, it's okay to have parties in graveyards. But German graveyards are somber affairs. There is one next to my office. What is a month, I think, as I march through it some days later. I feel my period coming on. I am keeping time in a way that's new to me. There has been no smooth transition from waiting for something to happen and it being almost too late.

There are, of course, baby graves.

When I am menstruating, the feeling is of extreme power and also extreme fragility. I want to hold myself in my fist, which may have crushed bones, but gently. Marching through the graveyard near my office, I think about how eggs, when pressure is applied to both the top and the bottom, will not break. In spite of myself and the fastidiously tender care I take, there is no accounting for anyone else. It is like being on the motorway. My body is performing magic, and this is how I want to be seen: with wonder and reverence. I want people to believe I am in greater pain than I am. I will be folded, via this awe and a little pity, into an affective space inaccessible to me for the rest of the month.

In the graveyard, an unkempt tombstone belonging to a Hermann Wolf brings a small tear to my eye. You like to go running at night. I'm a wolf, you've said, biting, and you're an antelope. I realise that a lot of what we've been doing is thinking about and referring to consuming one another. A very beautiful rose bush grows up the crumbling wall behind the wolf tombstone, and it makes me weep fully and laugh at the same time. The laughter is for the benefit of a weathered stone angel who observes me through blind, mossy-eyed sockets.

PMS, I say to the stone angel.

*

A once-estranged friend is saying: I have a special tree stump in the forest behind my house where I sit after a good storm, breastfeeding. I feel like mother nature. She drinks her tea and rights the wonky heart-shaped sunglasses on her baby's head. She shows me how she can spurt breast milk from one side of the cafe terrace to the other. Two things happen: a waitress comes out with a tray of drinks and steps right into the jet of breast milk. How does the tepidness of the milk on her face and forearms feel? The second thing is that my friend's baby projectile vomits.

*

Another day, another cafe. Next to me are four adults and a baby. The adults stare spellbound at the baby, which is breastfeeding. It is like the breast is a part of the baby and not the woman. No one says anything. During an ayahuasca trip, my arm melted into the shaman's arm and was no longer mine.

A man who is not part of the baby group is saying to a woman: Her problems—where do you *put* her problems? In the last basket of *your* problems, that's where. The plan is *income*, and if the plan is income, you may as well release an album. I mean, if you fail or if I fail, we will *always* have our parents.

Not always, the woman says.

The man looks fifteen, but is probably older. He sounds French. As much as breasts fascinate me, their conversation piques my interest more than the breastfeeding baby. What would I put in my basket of problems? Am I in the last basket of someone else's problems?

*

Time folds itself in around me. It is as heavy as a weighted blanket. Weighted blankets don't fold, you say.

Of course they do.

That sounds quite nice then, you say.

It's not, I say darkly. But I have captured the essence of it.

I say: It is also like cycling along some river, let's say the Danube, headfirst into a gale. I am barely moving, and every tread of the pedal is one unit of now, and every next now could be the one in which I throw in the towel.

Fuck, you say.

Thank you, I say.

*

I write you long emails that I do not send. It breaks up the month of absence into four weeks of absence. I tell you things that have happened and things I have seen. In week two, I do a season re-cap. Throuple is such an ugly word, but being one was beautiful and

139

painful and funny.

My ex-girlfriend calls me.

How would you feel if we had a baby? Who?

Me and your boyfriend.

That is a very hypothetical situation, I say. He won't do it until you say how you'd feel. You having a baby depends on how I feel?

I don't like it either.

*

Today it's the size of a red currant, she says. Today it is a golden kiwi. An egg. A large tomato. A chocolate cake. A watermelon. A duck. Her gums bleed with all the extra blood that floods the body. Flossing is a massacre, she says, coming into her bedroom with a skein of bloody floss and a red shark smile. On this day, it is a banana.

She sends me a photo from the hospital when I am out running in the park. As I hyperventilate on the grass by the donkey enclosure, a drug dealer brings me water and several perforated pieces of kitchen roll. The baby is a grotesque alien. In group therapy, they suggest I am jealous. I am not jealous.

Ennui: It is summer. I walk past a man pushing a pram along the canal, and in the pram is a toddler. You could, right now, be walking on the grass, the man says to the toddler. But you refused to wear your shoes, didn't you, so now you can't.

Disgust: My nephew puts a snail in his mouth and bites down. My sister puts her fingers into his mouth and pulls it out. The shell is intact and he has snail slime on his lips.

*

Bipolar? my father says. He sounds excited. The best artists and writers had it. Suffering makes for incredible art. You're in the best company. He begins listing writers. You must read James Joyce. Think about Coleridge.

But what about you, I say.

I have never been depressed, he says. Not me.

Not even when I was fifteen?

That's very specific, he says. He hands me over to my mother and we exchange pleasantries. After five minutes I say I must do the dishes. My mother pretends she has not heard me and says she must go, my father has made scrambled eggs. I have a very clear vision of the plate he is placing before her as she says this, his eggs are so perfect, they have parsley on them, they have a splash of cream
in them, they have lots of butter in them, they are so so good, and this knowledge and the vision of the plate makes me so sad that I hang up before we have said the obligatory amount of goodbyes.

*

I'm worried, you said back then, it was summer and we were lying

141

beneath a tree, that you would've fucked anyone or anything back then. Even a tree. All this time we'd been having the best sex we've ever had. Paraphilia is sexual attraction to trees. I've never had sex with a tree, but the ocean has, on several occasions, made me come. Sometimes I am a mermaid on hard pebbles. Sometimes I wear extravagant hats and eat fancy cheeses on trains. Sometimes everyone wants me and I want everyone, and everyone is watching me all of the time, and I am running everywhere listening to jungle music, and I get a hand tattoo and blue hair, and my time moves faster than everyone else's time.

In the beginning, I have splotches on my stomach. The pills are too large to swallow. I don't recognise myself in the mirror. My glands are swollen.

01.02.22: Left breast sore. Hyperaware of peristalsis. Light sensitive.

02.02.22: Puffy face. Obsession with Elton John and Meatloaf.

06.02.22: Reckless spending, low energy, inconvenient reliance on memes.

24.02.22: Irritated by the sea. An inability to ride my bike.

It's reassuring, I said, because if nothing is happening, it proves it's not nothing.

You watched me eating a big, not quite ripe golden kiwi, forcing a little spoon under the hard white nub at the centre. It's funny how you're twisting your face up in the same direction as you're twisting the spoon, you said.

Which?

Anti-clockwise.

*

My resolve is as unyielding as an egg boiled for fourteen minutes. The yolk of the resolve is tinged grey and crumbly, but the resolve itself is not. I feel good and strong. I call your other girlfriend and arrange to pick up my spare key. I am very resolute.

Despite my resoluteness, I bring her a Tupperware of curry I made, and we admire her haircut. A month has been up for months. I have had at least three periods, and we have not crossed paths. I have passed many cemeteries and not found you at their gates. I no longer want to eat you. I believe you might be hiding behind the bedroom door. The way your girlfriend, who is my ex-girlfriend, casts frequent looks at it. The way the incense is burning. The way the bedroom door is shut. You are on the other side, pressing your ear against it, listening, not breathing. I am afraid you will come out, and we will start gnawing on each other, which would be inappropriate in this setting.

I'm sorry, my ex-girlfriend says. She says: I feel resigned.

The half-eaten cheese sandwich, as if you'd left it in a hurry. With embarrassment, I think about all the times I washed your dishes in this apartment. I made you and my ex-girlfriend like kohlrabi. I think about the knife I gave you. I think about the curry I brought her. I vow to review my policy on generosity. I think about how it is probably good to put all your eggs in more than two baskets.

I want my knife back. I say that at a performative volume, and my ex-girlfriend looks at me and says, What knife? I believe you are still pressing your ear to the other side of the closed bedroom door. I take back my Tupperware with the curry I made in it. The inside of the box is pleasingly foggy, the plastic rainy with condensation. Holding the Tupperware to my body, I say goodbye, and I do not turn into a pillar of salt.

On the pavement outside, a tall woman wearing an ankle-length camel coat and clutching a ring-binder to her chest stops in the night next to me. Her coat brushes my shins, and I know on some level that this woman must be a parallel-universe version of me. She throws her head back and keens. Her keen is so hard and sharp with grief it rends the air around me, it stabs at my shell and cracks it, then grasps it in its bone-crushing fist. Can I help you, I say. It is like she is trying to open a portal and I am trying to close it. I put a hand on her forearm, but she will not be helped and cannot be grasped. She slips her arm away. I try giving her the Tupperware, but she is still clutching her ring-binder. I would like to uncook my resolve, but it's a permanent chemical change. Regretfully, I leave the wailing woman and go home.

Arlo – Natalie Harrison (she/her)

She worked all day in her room, perched at a small desk. She wore no bra, moccasin slippers with plush insoles. Occasionally, she would glance up at the diaphanous curtain and squint, trying to ascertain a noise, or a clouded image. She lived alone. She had no pets. No one texted her for over seven hours.

At lunchtime, she scrolled her feed and ate a tuna fish salad with minced cornichons on top of Triscuit crackers that crumbled annoyingly onto her lap, as if she had whittled a piece of wood. When her work was done, she shut the slim, silver lid of her laptop and took a walk around the neighborhood. The sun had just dropped, and the Christmas lights were already up on all the rich homes. A tree shimmered white and gold through an arched window. The air smelled of smoke. She zipped her fleece up to her neck and buried her mouth in the pocket of warmth. Her eyes were large and willed the world to come after her.

She thought of many things. Work. She fretted over a silly mistake. She thought of her loneliness as if her loneliness were a physical object that could be held. An airplane in the sky was blinking. She thought of its destination, imagined a tropical beach, Cancun, Bora Bora. The bells at Sacred Heart clanged as the hour struck, a melancholy, reverential sound that made her think of a man she had once been intimate with, a man with boyish looks and a chickenpox scar in the center of his cheek, who wore a little cross that glimmered atop his thermal shirts. When they talked, she would be filled with a certain, particularly intense feeling, a feeling that no longer belonged to her and was now sad to remember, the way a grown up recalls a childhood tradition that has died.

He had ended up choosing another woman to be with and she had made a fool of herself, crying over the phone and telling him that he was dead to her. He had wanted to be friends. She wondered if he was still with the woman or if it had not worked out after all. It had been many years. Perhaps, if she had been a little bit less herself, or a little bit more, her life would be different and she would not be here now, walking alone.

Around the corner, situated across the busy thoroughfare, she passed the graveyard, which looked haunted in the darkness, with fog levitating white above the large stone memorials. She imagined the people buried there, their bones, their eye sockets. She walked down into the gutter to make room for a man with two dogs splayed on a leash. The lights melted in the puddles. Overhead, geese were migrating south.

Back at her house, she clicked on the fire and sat down to knit. Her fingers were stiff from the winter air. She had been knitting the same thing for a long time, and she never really got anywhere but she enjoyed the task, and the idea of what the nothing in her hands might eventually become.

After an hour, she clicked off the fire and went to look in the fridge but found she wasn't hungry. The plastic containers keeping old food fresh felt scientific. She picked out a svelte bottle of wine and twisted open the screw top, glugged it out into a big glass. The wine was slightly effervescent and, in her solitude, she could hear it fizzling. Sitting back down, legs tucked underneath herself, she opened her phone and scrolled through her contacts, reaching a name and stopping. Arlo. She stared for a while at the name until the digitized letters began to wobble, and then she pressed the call button and lifted the phone to her ear.

Through the rings, she felt sick and faint. She watched the tiny bubbles in her wine streaming upwards, as if panicked, in search of freedom. He answered by saying her name like a question. She said hello. He laughed then and said that it had been a long time. She apologized. For what? He asked. He sounded sleepy and his voice was heavy, like water, and she had the urge to swim through it. She said that she didn't know. There was a moment of complete silence that gave her a chill. The room had become darker and certain items glowed.

Eventually, he spoke again, asking how she had been, and she told him she had been fine. Him? Good, yeah, he said. For the most part. Life, you know. Her saliva felt superfluous, she had to keep swallowing. He asked her why she had called but not in an accusatory way. She told him that she just felt like it.

This time of year, she said. Puts me in a nostalgic mood.

Remember, he said. What we used to do?

Yes.

Would it be nice if we did that again? Or would that be too absurd?

No, that would be nice.

They hung up and she went into the bathroom. The light was raw, and she could see the age in her face. She made an attempt to smile and then stopped. She felt her smile was the ugliest thing about herself. She took off her clothes, kicked them to a corner. She could only see down to her crotch, the mirror stopped there. She had dimples in her hips. She pressed her finger into her belly and watched how it gave way. She thought of another man then, a man she had slept with only once, who had fucked her in a hotel room and then proceeded to tell her that her body was too soft for his liking. He had made a motion with his hands to express how he felt, a squishing motion. He had come inside of her and she had to wait for his cum to fall out, which it did later, and had wetted her underwear. The grease from his hair shone evilly on her palms.

She took several pictures of her naked body. She sat on the edge of the sink, where one of her breasts was visible, then stood facing front, sucking on her finger. She scrutinized the pictures afterwards, deleted three, and sent one. Arlo responded with a text:

Fuck. You haven't changed at all.

I could take a bite out of you.

He sent her an image of his cock, hard, veins icy purple, his pubic hair dark and thick. The hem of his boxers was polka dotted. She gazed at the image and traced the shape of his erection with her fingertip. She was still naked, coated in goosebumps, on the edge of her bed with her toes curled around the bed frame. Her head was like a balloon released into the atmosphere, about to pop. He called her back. He told her how much he liked the shape of her body. He compared her to a bend in the river. He expressed a yearning to kiss her, to taste her. She closed her eyes and listened, ingesting his words. A feeling from beyond surfaced and she brought it forth, reeling it out like a fish from the sea.

He told her that he had thought of her over the years and had missed her company. She told him, very sincerely, with a choke in her voice, that she loved him. He told her to lie down, to lie back, to imagine that he was there, with his fingers deep inside of her, and she obeyed, touching herself along to the rhythm of his words. She came loudly into the phone. She took a moment to recoup, and then illustrated a vulgar scenario involving giving him head in a public setting, and he exhaled, painfully, and the silence returned.

She could hear the wind scream outside and she thought, over the line, a woman's voice, but it could have also been a door opening, or the television. Arlo cleared his throat and asked about her Christmas plans. She felt stunned by this question, it felt too personal, and if she were to reveal her plans—or her lack of plans—wouldn't he be able to know what he had long ago done to her?

With a guarded scoff, she told him that she would probably be drunk over the course of the holidays, and he laughed and said he wished he could do the same. She did not ask him why he couldn't. She imagined them drunk together, sunk in the center of the couch, listening to the jingle bells as the horse-drawn sleighs went by, carrying families with small, gleeful children.

She pulled on her clothes and walked back out to the living room. She felt withered and her eyes burned. She drank some of her wine, which tasted yeasty. Arlo said her name slowly, as if he were trying to sound it out. She could remember, very distinctly, the way her life had changed when he came into it, and the hollowness that lingered when he left, like a spot in the ground where a root was unearthed.

She told him that she should probably go. He said okay. They both hesitated. She felt the desire to cry but didn't, she bit her lip until it hurt. The wine was warm but still petulant. He seemed to be trying to say something, but in the end, he just hung up. She picked up her knitting and pulled out the last row where there was a dropped stitch, watching the loops unravel so easily, one after the other.

NON-FICTION

A Mother's Unspoken Language – Anna Nguyen (she/her)

We're in the kitchen. I'm preparing dinner and she hovers over my shoulder. She wants to help, but the space is too small for two people. For the third time, she asks me what I'm making for dinner, gesturing to the slices of acorn squash, leftovers from when we made vegetarian filling for egg rolls.

I'm making soup, I remind her.

I'm losing my mind, Má tells me. It's because of my age.

She says these two short sentences often, whenever she's excusing her lack of hearing, her forgetfulness, her repetition. In person, the number of times these sentences are uttered seems alarming.

When I grow impatient with having to repeat myself to Má, I pin her with an annoyed look or repeat myself in an exasperated tone.

Aren't you listening to me? I ask, not waiting for an answer.

I'm losing my mind. I'm too old now, she says anyway.

I'm never sure if she's forgetting or if she isn't listening.

~

"Over the course of my life I have known less than twenty-four hours with my mother," is Beth Nguyen's first sentence in her memoir, *Owner of a Lonely Heart.* The sentence becomes an imperative for her to reflect on her mother's absence, their eventual greeting, and her own roles as a refugee, a resident, and a mother. Trauma caused by imperialism and colonialism forces its way into families, lingers, and inflicts lasting inherited pain.

It was her grandmother who decided to leave Saigon the day before the fall of the city. Her mother stayed behind. Or was she left behind Nguyen wonders. She didn't ask because to discuss the war was to discuss her mother. Silence becomes a strong force in these stories. Nguyen notes the idea of forgetting the past falsely promises the ability to move on. And, yet, it was not difficult to remain silent. Nguyen didn't have any actual memories of war nor of leaving. "I had the privilege, instead, of getting to imagine," she admits.

As one of many writers who aspires for a new way to imagine better worlds, I, at times, feel stuck with analysis. I look at my own mother and I try to understand through a language she does not share. Something that resembles a research paper formulates in my head and I realize I am not being fair to her. Maybe Nguyen is right when she does not see silence as a submission, "For many of us it can be a form of self-preservation."

Má has never used the word trauma, though I suspect she has it.

Or maybe she has and I don't recall. I don't even know the word for trauma in Vietnamese myself.

~

I have not seen Má in three years. The last time we saw each other, we had been in the same country. I would soon leave for another country, and it was a temporary farewell. But we speak on the phone every day. These telephone calls are a repetitive conversation. She tells me stories I've heard years ago, the details rarely changed. Some days, I humor her and listen. Other days, I grow irritable and interrupt her with a curt, "I've heard this before."

A small silence.

"Má quên," she apologizes. "Old people are like that."

I've returned and we're in the same country, and she's with us in Maine. Her hair is greyer—more white than grey—she cannot walk for too long, her joints ache for days. And she's stopped trying to understand English. At least that's what my partner thinks. Three years ago, she could carry on a conversation with him, with few translations as interventions from me. There used to be varieties in her explanations, her defenses, fewer pauses. He now waits for a verbal response. She has replaced chattiness with some head gestures.

It's her diligence in keeping up with her doctor appointments that prevent me from worrying too much. I'm actually relieved when I see shades of the mother that I grew up with as a child. At Mr. Tran's, the neighboring Vietnamese grocery store, Má clicks her tongue angrily at my lack of understanding her grocery needs.

She wants to make phở and bún. She needs two different types of noodles, but she throws at least four varieties into the small metal cart. Confused, I looked at the brand names and clarified that we were making a few meals and didn't need so many extra.

She snaps at me. She needs them. Her eyes flash the look of anger I once feared. I recognize this expression she wears when she refuses for her parental authority to be questioned. The fleeting moment of comfort passes and memories of her disciplinary action flicker in my mind.

I walk away. I busy myself in the frozen section, far away from her.

~

We're in the kitchen again, and I ask her to make đồ chua. Before I left the country, she had telephoned and dictated a recipe. I do not remember the measurements, but can recall the basics, enough so that what she's doing in the kitchen seems unfamiliar to the recipe I've been using for the past years. She rinses the finely cut carrots, now resembling matchsticks, in sugar and salt water.

You're not preparing đồ chua the way you taught me, I say, laughter in my voice. I don't remember this step.

What recipe? she asks. She doesn't look up.

The recipe you gave me. The only time sugar was involved was during the final stage, before the jar was sealed for the pickling process.

That doesn't sound right. Are you sure you remember correctly?

I wrote what you said verbatim, I answer.

Maybe you misunderstood. I said you could use sugar if you want.

That's not ¾ cup of sugar, I remark later. That looks like a few tablespoons at most.

You don't need that much sugar, she sighs. You should just use however much you want. She must think I am interrogating her.

But it was in the recipe, I didn't say.

~

Nguyen was nineteen when she first met her biological mother. She struggles with the label of mother. "Birth mother" is not quite right, nor is "biological mother," the latter which connotes an adoption story. There are times when she deflects to geography and calls her "Boston mother," though it too is inaccurate. She didn't choose the city by choice.

I have critiques of origin stories, as biology is often essentialized and reinforced by the language of blood, DNA, and genetics, all of which would be used for nationalism. But I understand what Nguyen gestures at when she says, "there is no way of getting away from our origin stories." Places and placemaking are important aspects of the narrative caused by forced resettlement.

During a meeting with her mother in Boston, Nguyen tries to ask her about Vietnam. Her mother responds, that was so long ago. Nguyen poses the question thirty years after their first meeting, and writes she sees her point. "Like my mother, I am less and less sure of what is real, what is remembered, what is necessary to believe."

I am unsure if Má forgets or if she is unwilling to speak from a place where there are traumatic memories. Perhaps it is a combination of both. I have rarely asked her what her life had been like in Vietnam. She might provide details through the stories I've heard for decades: chasing and threatening a neighbor around the village with a butcher knife after discovering he had murdered and cooked her dog; finding out that her boa constrictor had suffered a similar fate; her aunt's chatty parrot who snacked on chili peppers; her days working in the rice fields; her desire to learn martial arts and practicing it in the mountains. She doesn't mention war, but I know its destruction lingers in these stories as background, as history, as an unspoken detail. She had been a young girl when the war began.

Years ago in Arkansas, my partner and I were enjoying the phở she had prepared. She wasn't eating and focused on speaking to my partner in English. She told him how she witnessed a soldier who had stepped on a bomb and blew up before her eyes.

"I couldn't eat meat for years," she said, shuddering at the memory.

He and I looked at her, our appetites vanished.

In Maine, she tells him the story about her dog, her snake, chasing people down the street. But she doesn't share the story about the fate of the soldier. I never hear her share the story again.

I've read somewhere that both needless repetition and forgetting are reflections of trauma. I am curious why she chooses to tell certain stories over others. Was there a momentary lapse in suppression?

I don't ask Má. Nor do I try to analyze.

~

Má has been walking with a cane for several years now. She relies on it more than ever.

We were crossing a busy street. I gently hooked my arm with her other hand to guide her, fearing drivers were unkind.

"Let go," she admonishes. "People will think I'm disabled."

~

We spend a lot of time watching an old TVB wuxia drama, the 1983 version of *Thần điêu đại hiệp*. She seems excited to watch it, exclaiming she hadn't seen it for nearly five years.

We watched the beginning together in Watertown three years ago, I remind her.

She can't confirm my statement. She doesn't remember.

The famed theme song by Teresa Cheung fills the living room.

The drama is long at 50 episodes. We spend almost a week watching it all, from beginning to end.

She stares at the screen and narrates what is happening.

Where is that scene when Quách Tĩnh tells Dương Quá the truth about his father?

I'm on the floor, my back on the edge of the sofa, listening to the dubbed Vietnamese as I work on my laptop. I look up to assess the moving pictures.

That scene just passed, Má. You can't hear? I'm concerned. She's been saying her hearing is going.

I can't hear so well, she always says. But she remembers the storyline quite well it seems.

I turn up the volume ever so slightly. It doesn't help. What she doesn't narrate, she inquires about a missing scene.

She doesn't say she forgets. She thinks the scene had been cut out.

It's not the images she remembers. She is asking about the dialogue.

Thần điêu đại hiệp is a serialized story written by the late Jin Yong. Days after she left, I watched Wong Kar-wai's *Ashes of Time*, an origin story of some sort, featuring some key characters from *Thần điêu đại hiệp*. The bare bones of the story and characters are familiar, but there is very little action, a controversial choice for a wuxia story. His elliptical style requires knowledge, the viewer must do some work of understanding, to trace any remnants that may be from the original source.

The characters are not merely heroes or villains, a Jin idiosyncrasy. Wong paints them as very cruel people, the cruelty enhanced as they struggle to survive in the pugilistic desert. All of them are haunted by some sort of trauma and unwanted memories. They are going blind or suffering from memory loss. A magic wine made by a former love promises no memory and no past, thus guaranteeing a new beginning.

In one scene, an ailing but luminous Maggie Cheung pines for Ouyang Feng, played by the late Leslie Cheung, moments before she passes away. She's barely a character in Jin's story, but we know she marries his elder brother. In Wong's explanation, she did so as a ruthless response to Ouyang Feng's arrogance. It's an action that she regrets but is too proud to reach out to him.

Huang Yaoshi, played by Tony Leung Ka-fai, poignantly tells her, "Some things don't need to be said." At the time, she needed to hear it, Maggie's nameless character explains.

I have only told Má her children love her once. All of us were in Arkansas, when my father suffered a fatal second stroke. We were very focused on his failing health, and Má, who had been estranged from him, had reluctantly returned to help us care for him. She came back for us, her children, not my father. She complained that no one seemed to ask about her wellbeing. I recall deliberately using the word thương, connoting a sense of care. I mainly used it to refer to a sense of moral obligation, between child and parent.

I think she understood. Or perhaps it is more accurate to state she didn't say anything more.

When I am testing the boundaries of explanation, exposition, and references, I find myself thinking of *Ashes of Time*. I selfishly try to avoid explaining too much.

~

There's a craft lesson Nguyen imparts, in trying to cohere some messiness of her family's story. "I find that I am a writer, writing nonfiction, trying to keep some things for myself. Trying to figure out what is mine, what is time, what is mine to say, what are we doing with words when they begin with someone else?"

How to describe my relationship with Má without relying on some tropes of estrangement? Of intergenerational trauma? Of our inability to understand one another? When the answer is always colonialism, capitalism, and imperialism, how useful is my hesitant analysis in tracing these silences?

When I don't have answers, I simply allow the silences to remain somewhere. They don't disappear.

Requiem For a Girl I Once Knew – Rose McCoy (she/her)

I remember distinctly the first day we spent together, just us. It was a Thursday and I'd just gotten out of the psych ward on Wednesday. You, Tuesday. We were freshly recovered—or at least, that's what we were supposed to be. In reality, we were both a little more damaged than before, tangled in the trauma of white walls, bad nurses, and disavowed friendships—you know, the usual criminal culprits of attempted convalescence.

We listened to Phoebe Bridgers because you knew I liked her, and then we watched *Carol* and I tried not to kiss you and failed. I remember that, too: me sitting behind you, staring at your neck. I'm sure I brushed your hair away and kissed you there first, my lips brushing your skin tenderly before traveling to your jawline, your earlobes, your left collarbone. In a few gentle, slow moments my torso was bent across you, and Rooney Mara watched from a distance as you leaned back to give me access to your breasts.

I remember how your breathing changed and I, naïve and new at this, knew it to be arousal—but I didn't actually know that at all, because it wasn't true in the first place. You told me later, during one of those teary-eyed confessions that always seemed to come later than they should have, that the moment had actually had you trapped in the past—you'd flashed back to your terrible childhood and the things your father had done. You said you'd been trying not to cry. I wanted to cut off my hands and seal my lips shut with cement.

It ended up being okay, though. You didn't hold it against me. I know because before I left that day, you walked me into the living room, eyeing the creepy security cameras your stepfather had installed, and you held me. We swayed. No particular rhythm, no particular reason other than new love and just a touch of bitter resistance (I know that part because right before you let me go, you raised your middle finger to the corner of the room and smiled).

It wasn't quite a honeymoon phase, but those moments—those few days where things felt good and tranquil—were still ours. I cherished them in the week after, when you stopped answering my texts, and I tried not to be dramatic about it, but I couldn't help being worried and hurt after such a wonderful first day with you. I remember how my family and I went to some arcade, and both my sisters brought their friends, and all I could think about was how much fun we might have had if only you'd bothered to answer me about coming along. I wish I'd had the sense to figure out that those times, the regretful ones, would grow so much more common than the good ones, but I couldn't have known that then. I won you a stuffed llama anyway.

After a few weeks of what I so desperately wanted to call courtship, I stopped hiding the intensity of my feelings. I told you how it felt to burn with love and want for you over an hours-long FaceTime call, and you cried when you said that you wanted to feel the same way, you really did. But you couldn't, you said. You weren't made like that. You loved me, you appreciated me, you felt like there was a possibility of reciprocation eventually—it just wasn't now. I was just happy to hear that it wasn't an outright *No,* and I told you I'd wait as long as it took. That wasn't my first mistake, but it was undoubtedly the biggest—second only to the fact that I stuck to that promise until you cut me out by force.

I don't like remembering our ending. It's murky and muddled; it's messy and maudlin and miserable. It hurt. It still hurts when I'm foolish enough to think about it. And even though it was your fault, and more or less your choice, that we gave each other up, I can't help thinking about all those nights I said I'd never leave you. It leaves me reeling, because if I promised I'd never leave you and I did, doesn't that mean I abandoned you? Doesn't that mean I broke a promise that I'd once given with conviction thicker than my very blood?

I've learned a lot since that fateful Thursday, but this piece isn't meant to preach or teach or spout morals. It's not a lesson or even a warning (though it might feel like one on certain days). It's not even a crying out or a shout into the void. It's just a kind of quiet sadness, radiating regret; a letter to the girl I loved with my whole body and being, who didn't even have the decency to properly break my heart. If you're out there, Emily, hear this: I don't blame you. And while I do not wait for you anymore, there's a lantern lit on the towpath just in case you ever feel like coming home.

The Import Shop – Reyzl Grace (she/her)

What I remember first are boots and voices.

Most of the Russian import shop's customers see it in the summer or at the start of the Iditarod—an Aladdin's cave of matryoshka dolls and samovars that helps tourists imagine that going to Alaska is traveling abroad. The rest of the year, the clientele is smaller, but growing as the refugees pour in from the Union disintegrating seven hundred miles to the west. The shop *they* walk into is filled with tins of chicory and apricot tea biscuits—a pantry that allows them to pretend, for just a moment, that they haven't traveled anywhere at all. I truly haven't traveled anywhere; I'm just small and need a place to warm my fingers, and of all the places downtown to do so, this one is my favorite—the one I beg to go in and see.

To my parents, both of whom voted for Reagan twice and feel like they personally helped win the Cold War, there is something vaguely unpatriotic in this, but they indulge what seems a preschooler's natural attraction to colorful dolls and delicious biscuits, imagining it a benign and temporary infatuation soon to be corrected by their own grey vision of the Russian world. But I am too young to care about "soulless" apartment blocks in some proverbial Siberia. What is present to me is the Russian diaspora—a world of toys and treats and, most memorable of all, impossibly tall women who stamp the snow from impossibly tall boots and speak like the sea in the harbor. I'm sure men must have come into the store too, but they make no impression. It is those boots with the sharp toes and high heels, and those voices whose consonants glitter along their surfaces, while cold, deep vowels run in currents down below.

I learn later that Konrad Lorenz, whose work on the "imprinting" of newly hatched birds on their mothers made the

164

word a household term, initially thought that his goslings were responding to motion and attaching themselves to his boots. It would take twenty years for Gilbert Gottlieb to show that the object of the birds' imprinting was, in fact, the voice—a recognition and attachment that was essential to their natural development.

I could have told him that.

The bell on the door rings. Another woman walks in and meets the shopkeeper's greeting: *Здравствуйте! Здравствуйте! — Be healthy! Be healthy!*

***

It takes ten years for a voice I can't find in myself to arrive in a parcel of pirated MP3s, but still I can't quite recognize it for what it is. At fourteen, I have no understanding of the expectations I disappoint, no way to articulate how unheard I feel, no words for the thing I am becoming, so I pick fights with my father's politics instead. It is easier to tell him Star Wars didn't collapse the Soviet Union than to ask why he can't just let me love the things I love. It is safer to call trickle-down economics a sham and hurl quotes from Marx than to probe who my father finds worthy of compassion and who he doesn't. It is more comfortable to declare abstractly that mutually assured destruction was only an illusion of security than it is to face the reality of how willing he had been to sacrifice me for his principles. I haven't learned anything about the AIDS crisis, so I don't realize yet how many ways there might have been for him to let me die.

My mother senses it, though—takes me aside at odd moments when my father is at work to tell me about her years performing in show choir and what lovely people her gay friends had been. She always ends these stories with an invitation that, if there is anything I need to tell her, I can, but I can't figure out why

165

she keeps saying that. I have a copy of the Russian version of *200 km/h in the Wrong Lane* and a huge crush on Lena Katina. No one has told me yet how many ways there are to be gay.

My father is also worried about the wrong one, trying to coach me into becoming what I most fear. He can't perceive how his every effort to close a gap just pulls it wider as he confidently reassures me that each breakup is nothing because girls are all pretty much the same, as he nudges me to point out prospects that meet his hip-measurement criteria for womanhood, as he makes his own pass at male bonding through comments about actresses on TV without noticing how I am noticing my mother trying not to notice. For years he doesn't grasp that I call him a *capitalist* because I don't dare call him a pig to his face, and I'm relying on the phrase to autocomplete by association. But then again, I don't quite grasp that either. The voice makes all the difference, and in English the cadence of the word is too bouncy—musical even; it always sounds like a good-natured ribbing. Only in Russian, with the stress on the last syllable, can it be properly spat: *буржуа*. It is only in the *non sequitur* of his response to that—*androgynous eurotrash*—that I realize that both of our politics are about something else.

When he comes into my room later to talk, what papers over the rift is my t.A.T.u. poster. He thinks he understands—thinks he recognizes new colorful dolls that couldn't help but grab an adolescent's attention. But he hasn't listened to the album. He hasn't heard Lena's voice: *Это медленный яд, это сводит с ума / А они говорят – виновата сама / . . . / Мама папа прости — It's a slow poison, it drives me mad / And they tell me to blame myself / . . . / Mama, papa, forgive me.* He wouldn't understand it even if he did listen; he doesn't know Russian.

Not long after this, Reagan dies. My mother goes into mourning.

***

In a few years, I outgrow the album and the poster doesn't come with me to college. Instead, on my first night in the dorm, I stay up until two listening to the Russian exchange students gathered to smoke outside the building's entrance, just under my fourth-story window. They're from Khabarovsk and their vowels sound like the glow of their cigarette tips in the dark, which, in Alaska in August, is still light enough to see their chic stiletto boots.

In a week, those boots have the attention of half the American guys in the building, but they don't know Russian, either. In a month, I'm the one getting packed into the back of vans to come to the Russian kids' parties; I'm the one still secreted away in the girls' dorm in the wee hours of the morning. My roommates think they understand what I'm doing, but they don't. At two a.m., I'm up listening to Masha, whose voice was the prettiest outside my window that first night, narrate the life of Viktor Tsoi as she introduces me to my first KINO album. Tsoi's graveled voice is as bitter as the tea we're both nursing, and Masha's red-brown hair is spilling over her shoulders in nothing but her tank top. There are two things I desperately want to say to her. One I'm not brave enough to utter in any language. The other, which my just-say-no upbringing still won't let me form in English, comes effortlessly in Russian: *Дай мне сигарету — Pass me a cigarette.* In Russian, I am someone neither Nancy Reagan nor my mother would recognize.

In Russian, I'm developing a separate voice—higher, thinner, more inflected—in unconscious imitation of the speakers I'm talking to most: two Mashas, two Natashas, Olga, Nastya, Sveta. They find this amusing and tease me when I copy an expression or a tone that's particularly *девчачий — girly*. Then I laugh, too, and look down at the toes of their boots with a nonchalant shrug. *Я хочу говорить так же, как ты — I want to speak just like you.* This is true, but also much easier to say, in either language, than *I want to dress just like you, too.*

It's cold. I'm wearing a parka anyway.

*****

After graduation, I leave Alaska, tell myself that I can live without chicory and apricot biscuits—that I can wear men's boots. I keep playing Masha's old KINO records, but I don't speak to anyone.

Eventually I move to a city far away. I run an errand with my kid. I drive past a little storefront whose only sign reads simply *магазин — grocery*, but I don't go in. Not that year. Not the next.

Summers pass and the fruit goes to waste. Nights pass and my voice goes hoarse. Dreams pass and the ones that are left become more precious. In English, I reintroduce myself to all my friends. I go to the DMV and change my license. I go to the consignment shop and buy new boots—proper boots, with the pointiest toes and the highest heels I can find. All that's left on my list is chicory, apricot biscuits, and a moment to pretend I've never traveled anywhere.

When I finally enter the Russian grocery, the little bell on the door rings to announce me, and its metal reminds me that my own voice is still creaking like a ship's hull and my tongue is rusty. But there are no matryoshka dolls or samovars here because there are no tourists to sell them to, and when the shopkeeper looks up, she smiles as though I were any of her regulars—as though there were no question that I am who my response will tell her I am.

Здравствуйте! she calls, and, for all the years I've been inland, my voice comes back to me like the sea: *Здравствуйте! Здравствуйте! — Be healthy! Be healthy!*

ABOUT THE CONTRIBUTORS

- ❖ Adam Paxton (he/him) is a writer from Newcastle Upon Tyne. He is currently working on his first poetry collection and novel. He is an anxious and fearful boy. Twitter: @TheSuicideJones Instagram: @thesuicidejones

- ❖ Adele Evershed is a Welsh writer who now lives in America. Her prose and poetry have been widely published in journals and anthologies such as Every Day Fiction, Grey Sparrow Journal, Anti Heroin Chic, Gyroscope, and Janus Lit. Adele has been nominated for the Pushcart Prize for poetry and short fiction and Best of the Net for poetry. Finishing Line Press published her first poetry chapbook, Turbulence in Small Places. Her second collection, The Brink of Silence is available from Bottlecap Press and her novella-in-flash, Wannabe, was published by Alien Buddha Press in May.

- ❖ Alannah Guevara is a poet-wife and vilomah. She is the EiC of Hunter's Affects: a lit mag for deadheads. She has a good handful of words floating in the aether. Some places they call or will call home include *Revolution John, Rejection Letters, Toyon,* and *A Thin Slice of Anxiety*. Find links on Chill Subs. Find Alannah on Twitter @prismospickle.

- ❖ Alex Carrigan (he/him) is a Pushcart-nominated editor, poet, and critic from Alexandria, VA. He is the author of *Now Let's Get Brunch: A Collection of RuPaul's Drag Race Twitter Poetry* (Querencia Press, 2023) and *May All Our Pain Be Champagne: A Collection of Real Housewives Twitter Poetry* (Alien Buddha Press, 2022). He has appeared in *The Broadkill Review, Sage Cigarettes, Barrelhouse, Fifth Wheel Press, Cutbow Quarterly*, and more. Visit carriganak.wordpress.com or follow him on Twitter @carriganak for more info.

- ❖ Alison Hallie is an NB artist from out West, living in the East Village. Alison Hallie is a featured writer for Ethereal Magazine, studied Creative Writing at The New School, and they have been published by Everybody Press Review and Dream Boy Book Club. Alison Hallie is always in love.

- ❖ Allison is a published poet, writer, and visual artist residing in Nashville, Tennessee. She is currently working on a collection of pieces speaking collectively to a love story.

❖   A mass of tentacles and rose vines masquerading as a person, Amanda M. Blake (she/they) is the author of such horror titles as DEEP DOWN and OUT OF CURIOSITY AND HUNGER, dark poetry collection DEAD ENDS, and the Thorns fairy tale mash-up series. For more, visit amandamblake.com.

❖   Ambica Gossain is a 42 year old poet currently based in the industrial town Faridabad in India. Ambica is the two-time winner of the People's Choice Award by A.B. Baird Publishing, and to have her work chosen for three of their anthologies. Additionally, she was invited to be part of their exclusive anthology called *Like Frost On The Winter Garden* featuring thirty pieces by eight chosen poets. Her work has most recently been selected to be published In *Sunday Mornings At the River and Arboreal Magazine*. Her spiritual contributions to this journey have been in the way of a thriving Instagram poetry account @tryst_with_fiction and founding a poetry feature page @heartofquill to support and energize the large and diverse poetry writing community and pay forward the help and support Ambica herself received from so many along the way.

❖   Anna Nguyen (she/her/hers) had been a displaced PhD student for many years, in many different programs and departments at many different universities in many different countries. She decided to rewrite her dissertation in the form of creative non-fiction as an MFA student at Stonecoast at the University of Southern Maine, which blends her theoretical training in literary analysis, science and technology studies, and social theory to reflect on institutions, language, expertise, the role of citations, and food. She also hosts a podcast, Critical Literary Consumption, which features authors, poets, and scholars discussing their written work and their thoughts on reading and writing practices.

❖   Audrey Wu (she/her) is a high school writer living in Cambridge, MA. She edits for a variety of literary magazines, has been published in Curio Cabinet Magazine, and attended workshops such as Iowa's Young Writers Studio And Kenyon Young Writers Review among others. Audrey focuses on writing personal poetry to heal and when not writing, enjoys baking, crocheting, and binging rom-coms. You can find her on Instagram @notaudreywu.

❖   Betsy Merbitz (she/her/hers) lives in Chicago and has performed at several open mics, poetry readings, and poetry slams. She has been a featured performer in the queer music and poetry series Homolatte, at the independent bookstore Women and Children First, and at the LGBT Center on Halsted. She is a previous semi-finalist in Guild Literary Complex Gwendolyn Brooks Open Mic Awards poetry competition, and she has been published in the anthology *S/He Speaks: Voices of Women and Trans Folx* by Moonstone Press. She has a BA from Washington University and currently works as a birth assistant at a freestanding birth center.

❖   Charlie Wührer is a queer writer and literary translator from the UK. She lives in Berlin. Her writing can be found in literary journals, writing competition anthologies, on audio porn apps, read at events in Berlin, and on surtitle screens in theatres across Germany.

- ❖ Christina Rosso (she/they) is a writer, educator, and bookstore owner living outside of Philadelphia with her bearded husband and rescue pups. She is the author of CREOLE CONJURE (Maudlin House, 2021) and SHE IS A BEAST (APEP Publications, 2020). Their writing has been nominated for Best of the Net, Best Small Fictions, and the Pushcart Prize. Currently, she teaches in the humanities department at Moore College of Art and through Rosemont College's MFA Writer's Studio. When Christina isn't teaching or working at the bookstore, they read tarot and cast spells under the full moon. For more information, visit http://christina-rosso.com.

- ❖ Dahra Perez (she/her) is a Mexican Seattle-based writer who has recently graduated from DigiPen Institute of Technology to pursue a career in film and animation. As a passionate animal welfare advocate, she currently works at an animal shelter helping new furry friends find their home. She is working on her first Poetry Works Collection.

- ❖ Devon Neal (he/him) is a Bardstown, KY resident who received a B.A. in Creative Writing from Eastern Kentucky University and an MBA from The University of the Cumberlands. He currently works as a Human Resources Manager in Louisville, KY. His work has been featured in *Moss Puppy Magazine, Dead Peasant, Paddler Press, MIDLVLMAG*, and others.

- ❖ Devon Webb is a 25-year-old writer based in Aotearoa New Zealand. She writes full-time, exploring themes of femininity, vulnerability, anti-capitalism & neurodivergence. She shares her poetry online, through live performance, & has had her work included in over forty publications worldwide. She is an in-house writer for Erato Magazine, an editor for Prismatica Press & Naked Cat Publishing, & is currently working on the final edits of her debut novel, *The Acid Mile*. She can be found on Instagram, Twitter, TikTok & Bluesky at @devonwebbnz.

- ❖ Dorothy Lune is a Yorta Yorta poet, born in Australia & a best of the net 2024 nominee. Her poems have appeared in Overland journal, Many Nice Donkeys & more. She is looking to publish her manuscripts, can be found online @dorothylune, & has a substack at https://dorothylune.substack.com/

- ❖ E.N. Loizis is a Greek writer, who lives in Germany. Some of her stories and poems have been previously published in Maudlin House, pidgeonholes, Apocrypha and Abstractions and more. You can find her at https://www.instagram.com/enloiziswriter/ & https://thebffclub.substack.com/

- ❖ Grant Shimmin (he/him) is a South African-born poet resident in New Zealand since 2001. He counts humanity, the natural world, and the relationship between them as poetic passions. He has work published/forthcoming at Roi Faineant Press,

Does it Have Pockets?, The Hooghly Review, underscore_magazine, Remington Review, Dreich and elsewhere.

❖ Izzy Okonji (He / Him) is a Southern Nigerian artist of poetry, storytelling & music. He has works that appears in Brittle Paper, Bruiser Magazine, Midsummer Magazine, & forthcoming ones in Wasteland review, Hiareth Zine. He listens to music ranging from Nas, Kendrick Lamar to Seal, Brymo, Chris Brown—even Jeff Buckley. He has a special place for American musician Mary J. Blige in his heart.

❖ Jeff Presto is an author from Pittsburgh, Pennsylvania. He is a fan of all things horror and enjoys mountain biking in his spare time. His favorite authors include Chuck Palahniuk, Bret Easton Ellis, and Ray Bradbury.

❖ John Grey is an Australian poet, US resident, recently published in Stand, Santa fe Literary Review, and Sheepshead Review. Latest books, "Between Two Fires", "Covert" and "Memory Outside The Head" are available through Amazon. Work upcoming in the McNeese Review, La Presa and California Quarterly.

❖ Karen Keefe (she, her) was one of the editors of *The Parlor City Review*. Her work is published *Anima, Anti-Heroin Chic, Silver Birch Press, unstamatic, Poetry as Promised, Wild Roof Journal, POETiCA REViEW, Scavengers,* and the anthology, *F*ck the Patriarchy*. A selection from, *Aphasia Built Its Kingdom in Our House*, is forthcoming in the *Beyond Words* anthology, *My Greatest Fear*. She lives in Vestal, NY, with her husband the poet, Robert Guzikowski. She can be found on Instagram @dragonkkg and Twitter @karen_keef.

❖ Kael Knoxton Martin (he/they) is a writer living in Lansing, Michigan. He has been writing for seventeen years, and his work can be found in Celestite Poetry as well as Mag20/20.

❖ Kevin Foote (he/him) is a writer, teacher, and explorer. He was born and raised on The Central Coast of California, but now calls Green Mountain his home. When he's not in class with his students, trail running, bow hunting, and inviting friends and followers into the writing process with poetry through social media and poetry slams. His poetry has been published in Beyond The Veil Press, South Broadway Press, Rainbug, Scavengers Lit, and Twenty Bellows Press where he also serves as an editor. You can see his published poems and works in progress on his instagram page, @feastsonfoote

❖ Koss is a poet, writer, and artist with publications in *Chiron Review, Michigan Quarterly (Mixtapes), Cincinnati Review (miCro), Spillway, diode poetry, Five Points, Spoon River Poetry Review, MoonPark Review, Gone Lawn, Red Ogre Review, Anti-Heroin Chic, San Pedro River Review, North Dakota Quarterly, Bending Genres, Beaver Mag, Sage Cigarettes, Roi Fainéant Press, Prelude Magazine,* and many others. Anthologies include *Get Bent, Beyond the Frame, Punk,* and several others. They've received numerous award nominations and won the Wergle Flomp

Humor Poetry contest. Their chapbook, *Dancing Backwards Towards Pluperfect*, is due out from Diode Editions in 2024. Find links to their work at: https://koss-works.com. Connect on Twitter @Koss51209969.

❖ A native New Yorker, Elgin Award winner LindaAnn LoSchiavo is a member of British Fantasy Society, HWA, SFPA, and The Dramatists Guild. Current poetry books include "Messengers of the Macabre," "Apprenticed to the Night," and "Vampire Ventures," and "Cancer Courts My Mother" (February 2024).

❖ Linda M. Crate (she/her) is a Pennsylvanian writer whose poetry, short stories, articles, and reviews have been published in a myriad of magazines both online and in print. She has twelve published chapbooks the latest being: Searching Stained Glass Windows For An Answer (Alien Buddha Publishing, December 2022). She is also the author of the novella Mates (Alien Buddha Publishing, March 2022). Her debut book of photography *Songs of the Creek* (Alien Buddha Publishing, April 2023) was recently published.

❖ Lucy Rumble (she/her) is an emerging writer from Essex. Her poem 'My Nan, Remembered' won third place in the 2023 Tap Into Poetry contest, and her work is currently upcoming in Crow & Cross Keys, Schlock! Webzine, and Hot Pot Magazine, among others. When she isn't writing, she is trapped in the dust and darkness of an archive (or her mind). Find her on Instagram @lucyrumble.writes or at lucy.smlr.uk

❖ Mateo Perez Lara is a queer, non-binary, Latine poet from California. They received their M.F.A. in Poetry from Randolph College. They have a chapbook, Glitter Gods, published with Thirty West Publishing House. Their poems have been published in EOAGH, The Maine Review, and elsewhere.

❖ Dr. Manjusha Hari she/her is a poet based in Kerala, India. A teacher by profession and a Ph D holder in Malayalam language and Literature. She began writing poetry in her mother tongue as a child and has contributed a number of poems to national and international literary magazines. She also has two solo poetry collections issued in 2018 and 2020. And also she is a co-author of 5 English anthologies. You can access her poetry online at the instagram page @m.shewrites_

❖ Mykyta Ryzhykh is an author from Ukraine, now living in Tromsø, Norway. Nominated for Pushcart Prize 2023, 2024. Published many times in literary magazines in Ukrainian and English: Tipton Poetry Journal, Stone Poetry Journal, Neologism Poetry Journal, Shot Glass Journal, QLRS, The Crank, Chronogram, Monterey Poetry Review, Five Fleas Itchy Poetry and many others.

❖ Navila Nahid is a writer and published poet, currently residing in Brooklyn, NY. Her published works can be found in *Free Verse Revolution, Humana Obscura, samfiftyfour* and *The Dream Gods* anthology. She also has a social media presence on Instagram as @navilanahidpoetry.

- Natalie De Paz (she/her) is a bisexual Cuban-American babe (poet, improviser, and style icon) born and raised in South Florida. She currently lives in the suburbs of Pittsburgh with the love of her life, their dog, and their cat. She has a BA in English from Florida International University and an MFA in creative writing from Stony Brook Southampton.

- Natalie Lynn Harrison (she/her) has work published with Indigo Literary Journal, American Writer's Review, Cerasus Mag and Miniskirt Magazine, where her piece "Fantasy Corona Commercial Land" has been nominated for Best of Net 2023. She lives in Sacramento, California with her husband and daughter.

- Reyzl Grace is a poet, essayist, and translator working in English and Yiddish. Her writing has been nominated for the Pushcart Prize, named as a finalist for the Jewish Women's Poetry Prize, and featured in *Room*, *Rust & Moth*, the *Times of Israel*, and other publications. She serves as an editor for both *Psaltery & Lyre* and *Cordella Magazine,* in addition to her work as a teen services librarian in Minneapolis. You can find more of her at <u>reyzlgrace.com</u> and on Twitter @reyzlgrace

- Robert Pegel is a husband and father whose only child, Calvin, died in his sleep of unknown causes at sixteen. Robert writes about the fragility of life and the search for transformation. Robert holds a BA in English from Columbia. He is a Best of the Net nominee for 2023. Robert has been published in The MockingHeart Review, Backchannels, Door is a Jar, The Corvus Review, Fevers of the Mind, ZiN Daily and others. Robert lives in Andover, NJ with his wife, Zulma.

- Ronita Chattopadhyay (she/her) finds refuge in words. She also makes a living out of it while supporting not for profit organisations in India. Her poems have appeared in The Hooghly Review, Roi Fainéant Press and Howard University's Power: An Ode to BIPOC Excellence, Mystic Owl, Streetcake Magazine, The Afterpast Review, Renard Press and Akéwì Magazine. She lives in West Bengal, India. And she loves tea, mountains, travelling and books.

- Rose McCoy (she/her) is a lesbian writer from West Virginia. She has been published by Alien Buddha Press, Cathartic Youth Lit, The Passionfruit Review, Moonbow Magazine, and many more. She is the author of three poetry chapbooks, including WHEN THE WORLD DIDN'T END (Naked Cat Lit Mag) and G R I E F I S A N A N C H O R . (Maverick Duck Press). When not writing, she's probably questioning her life choices or mourning over something that hasn't died.

- Sarah Sands Phillips (b.Tsí Tkaròn:to, Canada) is a Red River Métis/British artist and poet. Her practice spans painting, photography, moving image, sculpture, and text. She completed an MFA at the Ruskin School of Art at the University of Oxford (2019). She is currently based in Tokyo, Japan.

- ❖ Sean Robinson writes in the Upper Valley of New Hampshire. He has been a professional fire breather, cowherd, and spelunker. You can find him on most social media @Kesterian

- ❖ Simone is a Pushcart-nominated poet living in Chicago and writing about their queer life. Simone has been published in voidspace, moth eaten magazine, and vulnerary magazine, among others. Twitter: @simoneapoetry

- ❖ Steve Denehan lives in Kildare, Ireland with his wife Eimear and daughter Robin. He is the author of two chapbooks and four poetry collections. Winner of the Anthony Cronin Poetry Award and twice winner of Irish Times' New Irish Writing, his numerous publication credits include Poetry Ireland Review and Westerly.

- ❖ Syd M is a non-binary Arab American poet and artist that seeks to share their experiences and capture nature's beauty. They have been published by Mollusk Lit, Moonbow Magazine, Qafiyah Lit, and more. Their favorite beverage is Turkish coffee.

- ❖ Taylor Bowman (she/her) is a Black poetry and fiction writer and public educator. She holds two degrees; a B.A. in Poetry and a M.A.T. in Elementary Education. Originally from Michigan, she won her first poetry competition back in her hometown at the age of thirteen and has been writing ever since. Her poetry has been published in print and in online literary journals such as the *Columbia Poetry Review*, no. 30, *Thank You For Swallowing*, Vol. 2, issue 5, and more. She currently lives in Chicago with her partner and two cats, while writing poetry and fiction, and educating public school kids.

- ❖ Wanda Deglane is a poet and therapist from Arizona. She has written Melancholia (VA Press, 2021), among other books. She lives in Glendale with her beloved orange cat, Nico.